WAGONS WEST

THE COWAN FAMILY SAGA – BOOK 1

Russell J. Atwater

Contents

Chapter One
Kiowas!

Bruce Cowan lifted his bowler hat and mopped the sweat from his forehead with his bandanna. In Boston, the hat had served him well, but the Kansas sun bore down on him like a furnace's breath. Bruce's long nose, which stuck out farther than the brim, already felt sunburned. He glanced over at his bare-headed son, Wes. Bruce figured his son's bushy blond hair offered about as much protection as his bowler hat.

No one had told the stout Bostonian he would need a wide-brim hat at the general store in Kansas City when he had bought supplies for the Santa Fe Trail. They hadn't told him a lot of things, like how sore he'd get riding a horse for six hours. And that the recent rain would leave the trail so muddy the wagon would get stuck almost every half mile. When that happened, Bruce tied his and Wes's horses to the wagon and pulled it out of the mud.

Bruce missed Boston. He had made a decent living for his family as a brick mason. Everything had been fine until Mathias Coruthers, the brutal leader of the shipyard gang, had spotted Becky, his eighteen-year-old daughter. Lois had been ailing and sent Becky to take Bruce his lunch, which he had forgotten in his rush to be on time for work.

Unfortunately, Bruce had been working at Mathias's house, laying bricks for an addition.

Coruthers, a middle-aged gorilla of a man with acne scars, had taken one look at golden-haired, green-eyed Becky and declared he wanted to marry her, then and there. To say no to Mathias Coruthers was a death warrant. He had killed men for looking cross at him. Both Lois and Becky had been horrified at the notion of her marrying the ugly gangster. Bruce had sat down with them at the kitchen table and explained that, if they stayed in Boston, Becky would have to marry Mathias. Out of that conversation had grown the situation the family found themselves in now, on the Santa Fe Trail less than a day out of Kansas City.

"Pa, what are you thinking? Your face is all pinched up like it gets when you're trying to figure something out," Wes said. He patted his spotted pony on its shoulders.

Of the four members of the family, Wes had taken to the adventure with a young boy's enthusiasm. Becky still brooded over having left her friends behind in Boston, and his wife, Lois, lamented having to sell their house at a dirt-cheap price. Luckily, Bruce had managed to put off Coruthers long enough for them to find a buyer.

"I'm thinking about Boston, Wes." Bruce glanced at the two wagons ahead of him.

The one directly in front carried his wife, Becky, and the family's possessions and their trail supplies. The oxen-pulled wagon ahead of the Cowans' belong to Jitter Block, his wife Nettie, and their infant girl. A milk cow walked behind the wagon for the sole purpose of providing milk for the baby.

The two families had met at the general store. When they realized both were heading out on the Santa Fe Trail, they had hurriedly decided to travel together. Since Jitter was from Kansas, Bruce had hoped he would be a wellspring of knowledge on frontier travel. It didn't take him long to realize that the Bible was the only thing Jitter knew anything about. The wiry, dark-haired man with a baby face had experienced a vision, calling his family to journey to California.

"Pa, I like it here on the trail better than in Boston. I like Paint. He's such a beautiful pony. I bet he can run all day."

Bruce chose not to discourage Wes's enthusiasm. It lifted his spirits. And, dang it, his spirits needed lifting. They were half a day out of Kansas City with maybe weeks or months of travel before they found a suitable place to homestead. In the back of his mind, Bruce counted on finding a plot of land in Texas. Hopefully, a homestead along a stream to furnish a good supply of water for a farm. He had always had a little garden in the back of the house in Boston. He felt that qualified him to be a farmer.

Instead, he found himself half wishing he hadn't agreed to travel with Jitter. The Blocks' wagon held the front position because of the oxen. Two teams of oxen could out-pull horses but moved at a ponderous pace that left Bruce exasperated.

"Pa, I'm hungry. When are we going to eat lunch? My mouth is watering for one of Ma's biscuits and some bacon she cooked up at breakfast."

Bruce pulled out his pocket watch from his vest pocket. "I reckon we can stop if Jitter is obliged to halt for a spell. I'll ride up and ask him." As Bruce pulled alongside their wagon, he called, "Lois, Wes wants to stop for lunch. What do you think?"

Becky and Wes got their blond hair from Bruce's wife. Luckily, neither one had his Irish red hair. Lois drove the wagon while Becky rode on the seat beside her, reading her favorite dime novel, which she must have read ten times since they left Boston.

Becky lowered her book. "Yes, Pa! I'm starved."

Lois shrugged. "There's your answer."

"I'll tell Jitter we want to stop," Bruce said. "Not that I can tell if his wagon is moving, at times," Bruce added as he pressed his heels into the side of his brown gelding.

Unlike the two draft horses hitched to their canvas-covered wagon, Bruce rode an older Morgan horse. Bruce didn't know the exact age of his mount, but despite his advanced age, the horse seemed fit. He had gotten the Morgan and the pony cheap from the livery stable. The two draft horses had been pricey, but he figured their strength would come in handy.

Bruce nodded at Jitter, who walked beside the leading pair of oxen with one hand on the yoke and an open Bible in the other hand. Jitter glanced up from reading. "Howdy, Jitter," Bruce greeted him.

The wiry little man lifted the Bible. "I've got a spare if you feel the need to get closer to the Lord."

Bruce had purposely not offended the man by telling him he wasn't a churchgoer. However, Jitter's constant urging for him to read the Bible had begun to dig at Bruce. "Nope, I just rode up to tell you we are stopping for a bit. My children are hungry. Heck, you know how it is, kids are always hungry."

"Sure, Bruce, I'll stop the oxen but we ain't going to be eating. That is, unless we're going to stay put for a couple of hours. Nettie didn't cook up nothing this morning. We ate in the restaurant beside the hotel. And she is as slow as molasses in January fixing vittles."

Bruce had hidden his disappointment at the ineptness of the couple so far. He realized he knew little about pioneering across the plains. However, what Jitter Block and his wife knew wouldn't fill a thimble. Between them, he hadn't seen a lick of cow sense. "Join us for some biscuits and bacon. Lois cooked up plenty this morning."

Jitter smiled. "God bless you, brother! I think the Lord must have sent you to help us get to Texas."

More like the devil sent you to keep me from Texas, Bruce thought but didn't say. He just nodded while he turned his gelding around. When Bruce looked back at his wagon, a mounted Kiowa on the trail met his gaze. Bruce closed his eyes, hoping he had only imagined the figure. However, when he opened his eyes, the man still stood in the middle of the trail, staring at the wagons. While his heart raced like a Quarter Horse in his chest, Bruce kept his horse at a slow walk as he headed back to his wagon.

"You look concerned, Bruce. Is something the matter with the Blocks?" Lois asked when she got a look at her husband's face.

Bruce considered telling Lois about the man watching them, but decided not to do so until the wagons stopped.

"Lois, pull up beside the Blocks' wagon before you stop," he told her and knew that his wife would ask him why.

She did. "Why beside them?"

"We got to share food with them. Nettie didn't cook this morning."

Bruce's wife shook her head. "It wouldn't surprise me if she doesn't even know how to cook. She ain't much older than Becky. I'm not sure hooking up with the Blocks was a smart idea, Bruce."

Becky glanced up from her book. "I know how to cook, Mama."

Lois guided the team of horses to the side of the trail. "Yeah, but that doesn't mean Nettie does. Maybe her mother didn't teach her."

Bruce didn't hear the rest of their conversation. He walked his horse to the rear of the wagon where Wes twirled a lariat, pretending to rope a cow.

"Pa, I'm going to be a cowboy when we get to Texas and settle on a homestead. I'll rope and brand our cows."

"Yeah, that's fine, son, but first we have to get to Texas, and second we have to find a good piece of land to stake a claim to." While Bruce spoke, he glanced down the trail. Nothing. The man had disappeared.

Wes turned in his saddle. "What are you looking at, Pa? Did you see a jackrabbit or a coyote? I wonder if I could rope one like it were a cow?"

Bruce shook his head. "Just looking, just looking." Maybe he had imagined it. No, he had seen him, and it meant trouble. "Come on, Wes, up to the front of the wagon. We're going to eat with Jitter and Nettie."

"Pa. Their baby cries. It drives me crazy. They have the milk cow. It can't be hungry all the time, can it?"

Bruce shook his head. "Babies cry, Wes. That's a fact of life. You cried so much your ma and I considered renaming you Crybaby. Now get on up front and help your ma unload the vittles when she pulls alongside the oxen."

"Pa, I don't believe I cried as much as you say. I'm fixing to ask Mama. I bet she tells a different story," Wes said while he reined his pony over to the left side of the wagon.

Bruce didn't register his son's words. His thoughts were on where the Kiowa man had disappeared to. Suddenly he remembered they had passed a ravine a little ways back, around where he had spotted the mounted man.

"Dad-blame-it!" Bruce willed the concern from his face as he did during a poker game. He walked his gelding up to where Lois had placed a platter of biscuits and thick slices of bacon on top of a barrel of crackers. He dismounted as Jitter and Nettie walked over.

"I appreciate your invitation to break bread with you," Jitter said. "May the Lord bless you."

"Where is the cry... baby?" Wes asked as he reached for a biscuit.

"Son," Jitter said. "We haven't asked for God's blessing yet."

An annoyed look flashed across Bruce's face. "Wes already said the blessing," Bruce said as he secretly winked at his son.

"Yup, I'm good at saying the blessing, Mister Block," Wes replied as Lois glanced at her husband and rolled her eyes.

Bruce sat so he could see the trail behind the wagons. He waited until everyone had eaten a biscuit and some bacon before he cleared his throat to get everyone's attention. "I have something to tell you all. Now don't get your bowels in an uproar when I tell you."

Lois gave her husband a hard look. "Is something wrong?"

"It could be... I saw a mounted Kiowa man, watching us back down the trail a ways."

"Kiowa!" Nettie cried out and promptly fainted against her husband.

"You frightened my wife, sir!" Jitter called out as he fanned Nettie with one hand while he supported her with the other hand.

Bruce sighed and fought to keep his temper. "It couldn't be avoided, Jitter. I had to tell everyone. I fear there could be more of them hidden in the ravine we passed. I do believe that's where the man I saw disappeared."

Lois pointed her finger at the wagon. "Becky, get in the wagon this minute. You too, Wes."

Wes glanced at his father.

"Do as your mother said. And hand me out the shotgun," Bruce ordered. He looked over at Jitter. "Get your wife in the wagon. And if you have a gun, fetch it."

"I just got a scattergun. It's for hunting jackrabbits. Shooting a person goes against God's teaching," Jitter stated as he turned a shade whiter. He lifted his wife and hurried to the wagon.

"Bruce, these people are going to be our death," Lois surprised Bruce by saying.

"I thought you liked Nettie?"

"I did in the general store. Look around. We ain't there anymore. And being kindly don't seem to amount to a hill of beans out here on the trail..." Lois paused. "What are you looking at?" She turned to look back down the trail and screamed.

"Wes, give me that shotgun, now!" Bruce shouted as he walked over to the side of the wagon.

Wes's head popped out from inside the wagon. "Here, Pa. I loaded it. Here's the bag of shells," the boy said, handing the items to his father.

Bruce took the shotgun from Wes and then slung the strap of the ammo bag over his shoulder. When he bought the shotgun, like Jitter, he had only thought about hunting rabbits. It had only been the night before they left Kansas City that Bruce had heard tales of Kiowas attacking pilgrims on the Santa Fe Trail. And he had been in such a hurry to load the wagon the next morning he had plumb forgotten to buy a rifle.

"What are you going to do, Bruce?" Lois asked from behind the wagon seat.

"Whatever it takes to protect us, Lois." However, the thought of killing another man caused Bruce's stomach to churn. He might not read the Bible regularly like Jitter or even go to church often, but he'd never been a violent man.

Bruce glanced at the Blocks' wagon. He didn't see Jitter or Nettie. "Jitter, get your shotgun and come out of the wagon." The man didn't answer him. However, Bruce thought he heard someone praying. "Dang it. Prayer isn't going to help us," he mumbled.

Suddenly war cries echoed off the wagons.

Bruce glanced down the trail and found himself facing a charging war party of yelling, rifle-brandishing Kiowas. Bruce quickly sought cover. The only place that looked even remotely safe was under the wagon. He dove to the ground and crawled under the wagon as rifle bullets kicked up dirt near him. Once under the wagon, Bruce lifted the shotgun and aimed at the man riding ahead of the others. Knowing the range of the shotgun from hunting rabbits, he waited until his target almost reached alongside the wagon before he pulled the trigger.

The shotgun kicked his shoulder so hard he yelped in pain. However, the attacker fared worse. The blast from the shotgun knocked the man off his horse. He hit the ground hard and didn't move. A moment later, the Kiowas raced past the two wagons, firing their rifles into the canvas covers of the wagons.

Bruce reloaded his single-shot shotgun and turned around to face the Kiowas, who had stopped about three hundred yards down the trail. At that moment, the brick mason from Boston realized his family's chances of surviving the attack were slim to none.

Chapter Two
Trent and Patrick McLeod

Twenty-two-year-old Trent McLeod bent over the side of Tex, his Appaloosa stallion, to study the trampled grass at the entrance of a ravine that cut a deep gash across the rolling hills of the Kansas prairie. Trent's six-foot-two frame possessed broad shoulders and narrow hips that women loved, and men envied. His copper skin came from his Yaqui mother while his size, sandy-colored hair, and deep blue eyes came from his Scottish trader father. Trent favored a Sharps .50 caliber buffalo rifle. He always carried the big-caliber rifle in the crook of his arm. He packed a Colt Army in his holster and a bowie knife in a sheath on his cartridge belt.

"What do you see?" Patrick McLeod, Trent's younger brother, asked from atop the bangtail stallion he had chased for days before roping the big horse in a box canyon. Pat had inherited his features wholly from their mother. He was short and wiry, with coal-black shoulder-length hair and piercing brown eyes that constantly moved like a dangerously cornered cougar's eyes. Pat was mature, far beyond his eighteen years. He had practically been born with a pistol in his hands. He carried a double holster on his cartage belt. In each rested two lightweight .36 caliber Colt Navy revolver. When the occasion demanded, Pat would draw the Colts so fast they seemed to appear in his hands by magic. He carried a smaller hunting knife in his sheath with a seven-inch blade and handle wrapped in rawhide. He could throw it twenty feet and hit the bullseye each time.

Trent straightened up in the saddle. "Unshod pony tracks, twenty at least. Kiowas, I reckon."

"The ravine leads to the Santa Fe Trail," Pat stated. "Should we mosey on to Independence, Missouri, and look for work or see what the Kiowas are up to?"

Trent lifted his Boss of the Plains hat and ran his fingers through his thick golden hair. "Well, they sure as blazes ain't headed to California," he said in a Texas drawl that had a slight Scottish brogue.

"Reckon you got them pegged," Pat said as his mustang turned in circles, eager to be on the move. "Calm down, Leo," Pat added as he rubbed the big horse's shoulder. "The Kiowas are hunting wagons, I suppose."

"If it's a big wagon train, there might be work for us," Trent said while he straightened his hat.

His brother, Pat, shunned hats of any form. He wore the traditional Yaqui cloth headband and kept his glossy black hair shoulder length. Pat said he wore his hair in this fashion to honor his mother's people. Pat nodded. "It would be good to earn wages as we head back to Texas."

"We could catch a bullet for our efforts from these Kiowa Black Legs," Trent reminded his brother.

Pat chuckled. "When did the threat of gunplay ever stop us, Trent?"

"Never."

"Then we better get a move on before those Kiowas corner some settlers," Pat said as he gave Leo free rein. The big black and white spotted stallion tossed his head while he proceeded to descend into the ravine etched out of rock by rainwater over eons of time.

The two brothers had not spent any time with Yaquis. They had traveled with their Scottish father, Roger McLeod, and mother, Juanita, throughout northern Mexico and Texas. They had traveled from one outpost to another as Roger McLeod sold an assortment of weapons and tools to whoever had hard cash or something worthwhile to trade. However, that didn't mean the brothers hadn't received Yaqui training. Their mother had taught them to hunt, track, and ride at an early age. While Roger McLeod had trained them to shoot and handle various firearms, along with the military tactics he had learned while in the King's Scottish Regiment and how to read.

Trent had taken to the long gun. If he could see it, he could kill it with his Sharps. Although the Sharps was a single-shot rifle, Trent had become so proficient at reloading that he made it appear he was shooting a Winchester lever-action rifle. Not quite as quick on the draw as his younger brother, Trent had proven he could hold his own against gunslingers in a duel.

The brothers heard the shots before they reached the rim of the ravine. When they spilled onto the Santa Fe Trail, the twenty Kiowas had already made one pass at the two wagons. The warriors were milling around, getting ready for another charge, when Trent and Pat urged their horses into a gallop.

As they raced toward the two wagons, Trent dropped his reins and steadied the Sharps with both hands. He aimed at the man wearing the longest feather head dressing, knowing from experience that he was the war chief.

The boom of the buffalo rifle coincided with the war chief toppling off his pony. The startled Kiowas glanced at the two men charging toward the wagon with sudden respect. Instead of attacking, they milled their horses around their fallen leader.

Pat's big mustang reached the wagons first. "Anyone hurt?"

Bruce peeked out from under the wagon. His eyes were white with fear.

"Anybody hurt?" Trent asked as he stopped his Appaloosa alongside Pat's mustang.

"I... I don't know." Bruce finally found his voice. "Lois! Becky! Wes!"

"Are they gone?" his wife answered.

"Pa," Wes said. "You killed one. I saw him fall."

Bruce crawled out from under the wagon. "No, they are still here. But we have help."

"I'm scared, Pa," Becky said as she stuck her head out the front of the wagon.

Trent smiled when he spotted the girl. "Howdy, miss. Don't worry, my brother and I will take care of them. No need to be scared."

Becky stiffened. "Well, stranger, I'm not really scared. Just concerned for my father's safety."

Pat nodded toward the group of Kiowas. "Trent, quit eyeballing the pretty girl and put another of the Kiowas in the dirt. They're getting ready to charge. Shoot the one on the sorrel. I reckon he's the leader now."

"Excuse me, miss. I better do as my brother asks, or you might catch a stray bullet," Trent said as he turned in the saddle, raised the Sharps to his shoulder, and fired without seeming to aim.

"You got him," Pat confirmed as the man on the sorrel pitched forward off his horse.

"Of course I did," Trent said. He turned back and winked at Becky. "I never miss a shot," he added while reloading the rifle.

"Hmm, so you say," Becky responded curtly.

"Get back in the wagon and hunker down!" Bruce ordered. He looked up at Trent. "That's some fancy shooting. But will it stop the attack? They have only lost three."

Trent nodded. "Yup, if there's one thing a Kiowa fears, it's a buffalo rifle." Trent glanced over at Pat. "However, should they charge, Pat will blaze away with his Colt Navies, and at pistol range, he doesn't miss.

"You boys seem to know a lot about Kiowas," Bruce said while he intently watched the group of men who seemed stunned Trent had killed another of them from such a distance. "But if you don't mind my saying, he looks like one," Bruce said with a nod toward Pat.

"We're brothers. Our mother was a Yaqui and our father Scottish," Trent said. "My name is Trent, and I take after my father, while Pat takes after our mother."

"Dang, I would have never in a blue moon guessed you're brothers," Bruce said, still watching the milling band of Kiowa. "By the way, I'm Bruce Cowan. My wife, Lois, and my children, Becky and Wes, are in the wagon.

Pat nodded. "Glad to make your acquaintance."

Trent tipped his hat. "Likewise, here." He glanced at the Kiowas. "Should I kill another one?" he asked no one in particular.

"I don't abide by killing unless I'm forced to," Bruce said. "Wait and see if they start to charge."

Trent sighed. "It could be dangerous. If they're determined, some will reach the wagon, shooting for all they're worth."

"Yeah, but killing them from such a distance seems... seems almost like murder," Bruce said.

"You must be from back east," Pat said.

"Boston."

"Well, Mister Cowan..." Trent started

"Call me Bruce."

Trent nodded. "Bruce, we're less civilized out west. Sometimes it's shoot first to stay alive. And this qualifies as one of those times."

"Trent, they're packing the two dead chiefs on their horses," Pat said as his brother raised his rifle to his shoulder.

Trent lowered his rifle to the crook of his arm. "Yup, I see. They will want the one Bruce shot. They'll send a man with a peace lance to fetch him."

Sure enough, after the Kiowa loaded the two dead men onto their horses, one with only one feather in his headdress road up, waving a lance and leading an extra horse.

Pat responded with sign language. He glanced at Bruce. "I know a few languages, but the Kiowa tongue is too twisted for me. I just told the man to retrieve his fallen warrior with honor."

The three men watched the warrior load the last dead man on the spare horse. After he rode back to the group, the entire party cut a wide circle around the wagons and headed back to the ravine.

Bruce lifted his bowler hat and wiped the sweat off his forehead. "To be plumb honest, I thought we all were as good as dead when they attacked. And dad-blame-it, if you two youngsters hadn't showed up, the Kiowas would have massacred us."

Lois stuck her head out of the back of the wagon. "Are they gone?" she asked hopefully.

"Yep, thanks to Trent and Pat McLeod," Bruce said.

"Bruce, I hear the Blocks' baby crying, but I haven't heard a peep out of Jitter and Nettie," Lois told her husband as she looked across at the wagon beside theirs.

"Jitter! Nettie. The danger is over. You can put down your Bibles and stop praying," Bruce called out. Only the wailing of the baby answered him. "I'll go over and have a look-see. They might still be too frightened to make a sound." As he walked around his team of horses, Bruce could hardly believe their good luck that none of the horses nor the oxen had been hit during the shooting. When Bruce reached the Blocks' wagon, he pounded his fist on the side. "Jitter!" he yelled.

The baby wailed louder.

Growing suddenly concerned, Bruce climbed onto the floorboard of the wagon. He glanced beyond the seat into the back of the covered wagon. "Dang it! Dang it!" he yelled.

"What's the matter?" Lois called from the seat of their wagon.

"Jitter and Nettie are dead. They both took bullets. Oh, goodness, let me look at the baby," Bruce cried out as he climbed into the back of the wagon. A moment later, he emerged carrying the infant girl wrapped in a blanket. He glanced over at his wife. "She's fine. Just needs changing from the smell."

"Give her to me! The poor thing is an orphan!" Lois jumped down from their wagon and hurried over to the Blocks' wagon. "God must not have been listening to their prayers, Bruce. I'm just glad he spared us," Lois said when she took the baby from her husband. "Becky, you need to get down out of that wagon and milk the Blocks' cow. The baby needs feeding."

Trent tied his Appaloosa to the wagon's wheel and hurried around to the other side to help Becky off the wagon.

"Hmm, you are more of a gentleman than you look," Becky said with a sneer as she eyed his buckskin shirt. She walked over and lifted the milk pail off the hook on the side of the wagon while Trent stood back and watched.

"She doesn't seem to be smitten by your charm, brother," Pat said as he joined Trent.

"What kind of pistols are those," Wes said from the wagon seat. "They ain't Colt Armies."

Pat smiled up at the boy. "No, they are Texas Navies. Lighter than an Army and fire a .36 caliber shell."

"Wow, you know a heck of a lot about pistols, Mister Pat," Wes proclaimed.

"Drop the mister. I ain't that much older than you, kid."

"Will you teach me how to shoot?" Wes asked.

Pat shrugged. "It takes time, kid. Sometimes years to learn how to handle a pistol properly."

"Oh," Wes said with a disappointed look on his face.

Bruce walked up. "Wes, stop annoying the man. Go check your pony." Bruce waited until Wes walked around to the other side of the wagon. He glanced at Trent, who was watching Becky milk the cow. "What do we do about the bodies?"

Trent took a deep breath. "Give us a shovel, and Pat and I will bury them."

Bruce shook his head. "It seems barbaric to just put them in the dirt out here in the middle of nowhere."

"Do they have kin in Kansas City?" Trent asked.

Bruce shook his head. "No, I don't believe so."

"Then it would be foolish to haul them back to Kansas City!" Trent explained.

"Yeah, and I don't want to lose another day backtracking to Kansas City," Bruce admitted.

Trent and Pat glanced at one another.

"What?" Bruce asked when he saw the look on Trent's face. He had already noted that Pat's stoic expression never changed.

Trent sighed. "Bruce, I could honey coat it, but this is the time for blunt honesty." He swept his hand to include both wagons. With just two wagons and you and your wife, you ain't likely to reach where you're heading. If the Kiowas don't get you, the bandits will. I reckon you don't realize how dangerous the Santa Fe is for a couple of wagons. For safety's sake, you need to join a big wagon train. You'll have to backtrack just beyond Kansas City to Independence, Missouri. There you can hook up with a larger wagon train."

"Oh," Bruce exclaimed. "But I thought no one would find robbing two wagons worthwhile."

Pat spoke up. "The Kiowas thought two wagons were worthwhile. And so will the lowdown coyotes who rob and kill settlers, especially since you have horses. You need to trade in the big draft horses for oxen." He nodded over toward Bruce's Morgan gelding. "And get rid of the crow bait, Morgan. The boy can keep his pony."

Lois paused changing the baby. She looked up at her husband. "Is he saying we need to turn back?" she asked with a hint of desperation in her voice.

Trent spoke before Bruce had a chance to answer his wife. "Miss Lois, I ain't saying for you all to abandon your trek to wherever you're heading. But what I advise is for you to join a larger wagon train."

Pat nodded. "Yeah, there's safety in numbers."

Trent continued. "I'm sure if you go over to Independence, you'll find a good-sized wagon train leaving soon that you can join. And if that scattergun your husband is holding is all the guns you're packing, you need to scrounge up some more."

"The good thing is," Pat said. "You bought the right kind of wagon, the Murphy wagon, but you need to get rid of the team of horses pulling your wagon and buy two more teams of oxen. I haven't looked at your supplies, but I know without looking you need double what you're carrying. And don't worry, the oxen can pull more than a horse."

"And if there's one thing Pat and I have learned it's that, on a long trek, you can never carry too many supplies," Trent stated.

Bruce lifted his hat and scratched his head. "I'm sure everything you fellows are saying is straight as an arrow. However, I got to jaw with my wife on the subject."

Trent smiled and nodded. "Yup, I suppose you should bat the idea around with the missus. Pat and I will bury the couple and give y'all some space to figure out what fork to choose." He motioned to Pat. "Burial detail, Yaqui."

"You dig the first grave, Paleface."

The banter between the two brothers brought a smile to Bruce's solemn face.

Lois looked up as she finished changing the baby, and Bruce walked over. "Should we go back as they say?"

"Yes, I guess we need to join a big wagon train. You heard what Trent and Pat said. We would never make it alone," Bruce said. "I think they're right."

Lois sighed. "Maybe we should have stayed in Boston?"

"And have Becky marry that ugly thug? What kind of life would that be for her?"

"Well, she wouldn't have to worry about getting scalped by Kiowas. Or abducted by bandits and suffer God knows what atrocities!" Lois replied.

"Lois, if we join a large wagon train, we'll be safe," Bruce declared.

Lois shook her head. "Will we now?"

"What are Trent and Pat doing? I saw them wrapping Mister Jitter and Miss Nettie in sheets. Then they carried them out past the trail," Wes said as he hurried up.

"We have to bury them."

"But Pa, out here with no preacher?"

Lois spotted Becky bringing the milk pail. "Wes, fetch me the baby's bottle out of the Blocks' wagon."

Wes glanced at the wagon and rolled his eyes.

"Ain't nothing in there to hurt you. Now get," Bruce ordered.

Becky set the pail of milk down. "Mama, that cow is as ornery as a mule. She kept slapping me in the face with her dirty tail. And what are we going to do with the baby?"

Lois glanced at her husband. Bruce shrugged, and Lois sighed. "We'll see if there's an orphanage or a church in Independence that will take her."

"Are we going back to Kansas City?" Wes said as he brought his mother the baby's bottle.

Lois looked at Bruce for a long moment. "I reckon we're going to Independence, Missouri."

Wes turned to Bruce with a disappointed look on his face. "Pa, you mean we ain't going to Texas?"

Bruce shook his head. "No, we're going to join a larger wagon train in Independence and continue on the Santa Fe trail, maybe to California."

"California!" Lois exclaimed.

Bruce shrugged. "If we don't find a suitable homestead in Texas, we'll continue. We might not find a place before we reach California."

"Pa," Wes called out excitedly. "There's gold in California!"

"So there is."

"Can we pan for gold? I bet we could find enough to make us rich!" Wes added.

Bruce shook his head. "No, we aren't going to get caught up in the gold rush fever. We're going to stake a claim to a tract of land and farm it!"

Chapter Three
The Wagon Train

The Cowan family had been reluctant to go all the way to Independence, but the smooth-talking Trent convinced Bruce it was necessary. Bruce finally convinced his wife. The muddy streets of Independence lacked the sophistication of Kansas City. It teemed with men wearing beaver hats dressed in buckskins carrying rifles.

Near the stockyards, a group of wagons was assembling when Trent and Pat led the Cowans to the gathering point for the Santa Fe Trail.

"What do we do now?" Bruce asked Pat who rode beside him as he walked with the oxen.

Pat glanced back at the Cowans' wagon. He preferred Trent do the talking. However, his brother was trying to carry on a conversation with Becky, who had her dime novel opened and seemed to be ignoring Trent. "Strike up a conversation with one of the men on the wagons. Let them know you're heading out on the Santa Fe Trail and are looking to join up with a wagon train."

"Yeah, I guess that would be the way to go about it," Bruce said. "What are you and your brother going to do?"

Pat pointed over at the Frontier Saloon. "Drinking whiskey over yonder."

"I wish I could join you. I do love a snort of whiskey. But I can't leave the family among all these strangers. Will I see you and your brother again?"

Pat nodded. "Yup, we'll stop by tomorrow morning. Don't buy any supplies until we arrive. We'll help you gather what you need."

"That's mighty nice of you and your brother to help out. We already owe our lives to you," Bruce said.

Pat shrugged. "You would have done the same for us."

"I surely would like to think so, but to be honest, those Kiowa put my bowels in an uproar. I barely had the nerve to shoot one. Dang, it's a miracle I hit him," Bruce admitted.

"Tomorrow," Pat said as he turned his mustang around and rode over to meet Trent. "Miss Becky," Pat said and nodded at her. "Trent, my throat's dry. Let's go over to the saloon."

Trent glanced over at Becky. "Hmm, my brother is looking for trouble."

"Why do you say that?" Becky said, lowering her book.

"The Frontier Saloon has a sign over the door says No Indians!" Trent replied. "And look at him."

"But you're brothers," Lois said. "It's not fair for them to let you in and not Pat."

"But I look Scottish," Trent said.

"Come on, Paleface!" Pat said as he reined Leo away from the wagon.

"We all owe our lives to you boys," Lois said. "Will we see you again?"

"Yup, tomorrow," Trent said as he spurred his Appaloosa to catch up with Pat. Trent glanced over at his brother. "You sure you don't want me to go in and buy a bottle? We can drink it in that alley. The last time we visited the Frontier Saloon, it ended in gunplay."

"And the guy I shot deserved it. The sheriff cleared me. Ruled it self-defense," Pat said as they rode across the street.

"That was only because the man you shot was a French trapper who had been causing trouble for a couple of days in the saloon. You did the sheriff's job for him."

Pat shrugged.

"Okay, but try not to kill anyone." Trent shook his head as he tied his horse to the hitching post. "At least let me go in first. They'll think you're my scout."

Pat didn't respond, but he slowed a bit.

When Trent pushed through the swinging doors of the saloon, he found the room crowded with rough men and painted women in colorful, low-cut dresses. A woman danced on top of a table in the center of the saloon, caterwauling, as men seated at the table grabbed at her ankles, only to get kicked for their efforts.

"I've heard Kiowa war cries that hurt my ears less," Trent said as they wove their way through the press of bodies to an empty space at the bar.

The bartender, a white-haired man with a full gray beard, took one look at Trent and Pat and shook his head. "You two back again! You're not welcome."

"Nice to see you too, Gaby. How is that pretty Comanche wife of yours?" Trent said.

Gaby shook his head. “Okay, okay, just don’t talk about Rosario. Everyone thinks she’s Mexican. Dang it, I wish I never ran into you two on my way back from Topeka.”

“Gaby, you know darn well that if Pat and I hadn’t stumbled upon you and your... your wife, the Kiowas would have had your scalps on their poles,” Trent said. “Now, hush up and give us some whiskey.”

“Just don’t kill anyone this time,” Gaby said as he reached under the bar. He brought out a bottle.

“Firewater. Just what I need,” Pat said.

Gaby glanced at Trent and rolled his eyes.

Trent shrugged. “I don’t have any control over him. Anyway, you should take down the sign over the door. Pat doesn’t like it.”

“Here, it’s on me. Drink up and leave,” Gaby said as he poured them both a shot glass of whiskey.

“What are you staring at?” Trent asked as he realized Pat's attention had wandered.

Pat nodded at a burly, bearded man. “That man wearing the beaver hat is stalking the bald man in the red plaid shirt.”

Trent shook his head. “Pat, how do you know? They just walked through the door. Maybe they’re friends and an old beaver hat is following his friend into the saloon for a whiskey.”

“Nope,” Pat said as he pushed off from the bar to face the two men as they approached the bar.

“Digger Johnson! Time to die!” the man in the beaver hat yelled as he dug for his cannon.

Pat drew and fired his right pistol.

"Dang it! My gun hand!" the man in the beaver hat screamed as his Colt Dragoon fell to the floor.

The noise in the saloon stopped except for the man holding his hand and moaning.

"Buster Cooper! You lowdown polecat!" the bald man said as he turned around and immediately realized what had occurred. He glanced over in time to see Pat twirl his pistol back into his holster.

"You stole my woman! I told you I was gonna kill you!" Buster said through clenched teeth.

"I didn't steal her. She left you. The bald man glanced around until his eyes found who he was looking for. "Tom, you and Matt get him out before I put him out of his misery."

"Sure, Mister Digger."

The two men also wore red plaid shirts. They hurried over and lifted Buster to his feet.

"I ain't finished with you, Digger!" Buster shouted as the two men forced him through the crowded saloon and out the door.

Digger walked over to where Pat and Trent stood, each holding a shot glass of whiskey. "Well, are you going to look at it all day or drink it?" the bald man asked.

Trent and Pat glanced at each other, and then tossed the whiskey into the back of their mouths.

"Whoa! That's rotgut," Trent said and shook his head.

Pat's facial expression didn't change as he swallowed his whiskey. He nodded at Digger. "My brother doesn't like firewater as much as I do."

"Brothers? You two are blood brothers?"

Trent shook his head. "Nope. Same ma. Same pa. Anyway, I would never cut myself and mingle my blood with another man's."

"You two are brothers."

Instead of answering, Trent and Pat turned back to the bar. "Hit us again, Gaby," Trent said.

"Okay, but this one you're paying for," Gaby said as he pulled the bottle from under the bar again.

"No," Digger Johnson said. "I'm buying the brothers a drink."

Trent turned to face the bald man. "Thanks. We're low on funds, so your generosity is most welcome."

"I've seen some fast draws in my day, but you put them to shame," Digger said as he stared at Pat's pistols. "I'm not familiar with those. What are they?"

Pat turned around and drew his right pistol. "It's a Colt Navy."

Digger nodded. "Why did you step into the fray?"

"I just don't like sneaky shooters, mister," Pat said.

"You sound like a Texan with a British accent. You both have that strange drawl," Digger said. He nodded at Pat. "And it's downright strange coming from your mouth."

Trent shrugged. "That's because we spent most of our lives traveling through Texas, and our father spoke with a Scottish brogue."

"Are you any good with the buffalo rifle you're holding?" Digger asked Trent.

"I do all right," Trent said.

"Mister, don't let him fool you. If Trent can see it, he can shoot it. He killed a couple of Kiowas today at five hundred yards, and one of them while riding," Pat said reluctantly when Trent didn't elaborate. He didn't like to be the spokesperson since people typically dismissed what he had to say.

"Hmm, I might have a job for you two. Come by the mercantile where the wagon train is gathering tomorrow, and we'll jaw about it. Right now, I'm gonna play some poker."

Trent nodded. "Thanks."

Pat turned back to the bar without comment.

"It looks like helping the Cowans might land us a job on the same wagon train they'll travel on."

"I'm glad we're going to get paid for accompanying the wagon train because you had already made up your mind to go," Pat said.

"You know I hate you knowing what I'm going to do before I even do it," Trent complained.

"If you boys are going to get into a family squabble, take it outside," Gaby said.

Trent shook his head. "No, we'd rather stay and break up your tables during a fight. Maybe get the entire saloon fighting."

Gaby held up his hands. "Okay, take the bottle and leave. And I hope you go all the way to California with Digger Johnson 'cause I don't want to see you back here anytime soon."

"Gaby, for an ugly old coot, you're a decent man," Trent said as he grabbed the bottle Gaby slid toward him.

"If that's your way of complimenting me, you need to work on it."

Trent and Pat headed for the door. Several men gave Pat hard looks, but having witnessed his skill with a pistol, no one confronted the brothers as they made their way to the door.

Trent headed for the alley beside the bar. “Hey, we did well. You didn’t kill anyone. We probably got a job. And that old coot gave us a bottle of whiskey,” Trent said as he uncorked the bottle. He took a big swig and passed the bottle to Pat. “We shouldn’t drink so much that we can’t find our way to the stable. I hate sleeping in an alley.”

Chapter Four
The Mercantile

Trent reined in his Appaloosa and stood up in the stirrups. "They're busy as beavers, brother."

"Stop looking for Becky. We need to meet with Digger Johnson and find out if we have a job," Pat said as he stopped his nervous mustang beside Trent.

Trent nodded over at a large storefront. The painted sign hanging from the eve of the store said Johnson's Mercantile. "That's not difficult. His last name is Johnson, right?"

"Hmm, so he's running freight by wagon train to Texas and California," Pat said. "And judging from the men wearing red plaid shirts loading those wagons, I'd say he's got twenty wagons in the train."

Trent moved his finger as he counted silently. "I count thirty wagons. So that makes him the wagon master. It looks like he's got a slew of men working for him. Why does he need us?"

"He doesn't. He needs our guns. He'll hire us to guard the wagons, well, his wagons. I'm not so sure about the other ten," Pat said.

"If the Cowans are part of the wagon train, I'm certainly going to protect them also," Trent said.

"No doubt," Pat said. "No doubt."

Trent shook his head. “It’s not just about the girl. One of these days, Pat, I’m going to give you a good whipping.”

“You haven’t been able to lick me since I turned fourteen,” Pat replied.

“Let’s mosey on down to the store and see if we can locate Digger.”

Two oxen-pulled wagons were taking on supplies from the porch of the mercantile when the brothers rode up to the hitching post.

“Trent! Pat!” Wes shouted from the seat of one of the wagons. He held a big licorice stick in his right hand. His lips had turned black from licking the candy. "Are you two going on the wagon train with us?”

“Maybe,” Trent said. “Ah, where’s your sister?”

“She’s in the store looking at dresses. I tried to get Pa to buy me a pistol, but he refused. How can I learn to shoot if I don’t have a pistol of my own?” Wes declared.

Trent nodded. “I’ll see if I can talk him into buying one for you to practice with.”

“Would you? That’s swell,” Wes said as Trent and Pat climbed onto the porch.

Pat walked over and looked at the supplies two men were loading into the wagons. The door to the mercantile opened. Both Trent and Pat glanced around.

“Boys, I’m sure glad to see you,” Bruce said. “I got some expert help from Mister Digger on buying supplies. Since we’re joining his wagon train, he wanted to make sure I didn’t run out of necessities. Are you looking over my purchases to make sure I got the right stuff?”

"No, we're making sure these two load everything they're supposed to," Trent said.

Bruce shook his head. "Oh, I don't think you have to worry about that. Mister Digger Johnson came across as a sincere man." He paused. "Are you two by any chance joining the wagon train?"

Trent shrugged. "Could be. We ran into Digger last night, and he told us to stop by. That he might have a job for us."

One of the men loading the wagon stared at Pat. "You're the man who saved Mister Digger's life in the saloon!" he proclaimed.

"What?" Bruce said. "You saved Mister Johnson's life?"

"Pat sort of did," Trent said.

Bruce smiled. "You two have a knack for coming to people's rescue. That'll dang sure come in handy on the Santa Fe Trail."

"I guess we better make our way into the store and jaw a bit with Digger," Trent said and motioned for Pat to follow him. "You sure scared the crap out of Digger's man."

As usual, Pat's facial expression didn't alter. "Oops, there's your gal," Pat said, nodding over to the far corner of the store displaying readymade clothes. "That looks like a wedding dress she's admiring."

Trent touched Pat's shoulder. "You find the big bug and see if we have a job. I've got something I need to do."

"Okay, but she ain't looking at the dress with you in mind, brother," Pat said as he headed for the counter.

The clerk in the red plaid shirt looked up.

"I'm here to see Digger. He told me to stop by and jaw with him," Pat said. Pat's strange Texan drawl seemed to confuse the man.

"He's in the backroom going over the inventory list with his brother," the man said.

"Go fetch him!"

The man hesitated only a moment before he turned and hurried through the door behind the counter. The wait was short. Digger Johnson emerged, looking flustered until he spotted Pat.

"He's not a Kiowa, Doug. He's a friend. He saved my life last night in the Frontier Saloon."

"Sorry, Mister Digger," the clerk said and glanced at the floor.

Hmm, Pat thought, *he's got all his employees browbeaten.*

"Pat," Digger said and extended his hand. "Where's your handsome brother?" Digger asked as they shook hands.

"I'm the handsome one," Pat said, stone-faced.

An annoyed look flashed across Digger's face and vanished as quickly as it appeared. "Sorry, that was a poor choice of words. Where's your big brother?"

"Over yonder looking at wedding dresses," Pat said.

"I see," Digger said but obviously didn't.

"You said something about a job?" Pat said.

"Yeah, but don't we need your brother here to discuss it?"

"No," Pat said. If he was enjoying himself, he hid it well.

"Oh, all right. I need a couple of men good with guns to protect the wagon trains from two-legged varmints seeking to steal my trade goods. Are you and Trent interested in the job?"

"What does it pay?"

"Twenty dollars a month and board," Digger said.

Pat nodded. "That's reasonable. However, Trent said we can only accept the job if it's protecting all the wagons and not just yours."

"But *I'm* paying you, not the other ten wagons that joined my caravan," Digger complained.

"We either offer protection for all the wagons, or we don't take the job," Pat said.

Digger looked like he might refuse. Finally, he sighed. "Okay, you drive a hard bargain. I wouldn't want to play poker with you, Pat. No, sirree."

"Oh, and we don't do women's work," Pat added.

"Women's work?" Digger echoed the words.

"Load wagons, pull wagons out of the mud," Pat said. "You're hiring our guns, and we'll protect the wagons from any threat."

Digger hesitated a moment and then nodded. "Yeah, I suppose that's what I'm paying you to do."

Pat stuck out his hand. "Then it's a deal."

"Okay. If you and your brother need supplies for the trail, Doug will take care of you. He'll deduct the cost of the items from your future pay. At the end of the trip, I'll pay you what's left after your expenses," Digger said.

"What expenses?" Pat asked.

"You know, shells, clothing, weapons, or horses, should you need them during the trip," Digger said. "I'm not giving you free ammo, guns, or clothing. The only thing you get is food from the mess wagon."

Pat nodded. "Fair enough. Trent will not need any of those things, except maybe shells. Make sure your supply wagon has .50 caliber shells for Trent's Sharps buffalo rifle and .36 caliber shells for my Colts."

Digger turned to the clerk. "Doug, you heard him. See to it."

"Yes, sir, Mister Johnson."

Pat nodded to Digger before he turned and headed to the clothing department. As he approached Trent and Becky, he heard Becky saying, "The man I marry will be a rich rancher from Texas or a well-to-do merchant from Los Angeles. I want to go to Paris. They say it's such a beautiful city."

Trent shrugged. "Did you know the French are called frogs?" He chuckled. "I bet there's a lot of toads in Paris."

Becky shook her head. "What am I doing talking to a... frontiersmen! All you know is hunting beavers and killing Kiowa." With those words, she hurried over to where her mother was looking at canned goods.

"Sounds like the hen has flown the coop," Pat said as he slapped his brother on the back. "I guess you could say she's after a more colorful rooster."

"Did we get the hire?" Trent asked, ignoring Pat's remark.

"Yup. We're now officially hired guns for one Digger Johnson."

Trent glanced at Pat. "What? You don't approve?"

"I don't like the man. I'm not sure he's honest. It's just a feeling," Pat said.

"You and your feelings."

"Do you boys always dicker?" Lois asked as she and Becky walked over.

"Sibling rivalry, I think it's called Mama," Becky said with a smug look at Trent.

"I'm just glad to hear Mister Johnson hired you two to travel with the wagon train. I feel safer already," Lois said.

Trent tipped his hat. "Thank you, ma'am. We'll see that no harm comes to your family during the journey."

"Toads," Becky said under her breath as she followed her mother to the counter.

"I don't see wedding bells in your future, Trent. Well, not with that girl," Pat said as they walked toward the door.

Trent shrugged. "It's a long way to California."

Pat stopped. "Hold up. We need to buy a pistol for the kid. No matter what his pa says, he's going to need to learn to shoot. His life might depend upon it."

"You got money? Have you been holding out on me?" Trent asked.

"No, we get credit. Digger doesn't pay us until the wagon train arrives in California," Pat said. "And I want to grab a couple of bottles of firewater!"

The two men in red plaid shirts hadn't finished loading the Cowans' two wagons. Trent stopped and glared at them. "You boys make sure you don't miss something, or else you'll have to deal with me," Trent said as he lifted his buffalo rifle out of the crook of his arm.

"We know our job," the one who had identified Pat said.

Trent nodded. "That's good. I know my job too, killing when necessary!"

The man's face paled.

Trent smiled as he walked down the steps.

"Trent," Wes called out. "When are we going to get underway?"

"Soon," Trent said absentmindedly. He had directed his attention to a group of men gathered around one of the wagons. He walked over. "Howdy, pilgrims."

A huge man with a beaver hat and gold teeth stopped talking and glanced at Trent. "Are you one of the gunslingers hired to keep us in line on the trail?"

"First, pardner, I ain't a gunslinger. And second, Digger hired my brother and me to protect the wagon trains, all the wagons, from bandits. I'm not an enforcer of his orders."

"So you say," the big man said.

"Are you calling me a liar?"

"Jake, the blond looks tough with that buffalo rifle," one of the men in the group said.

Trent stood the Sharps against the wagon's wheel. "I'm tough without my rifle."

The man who had spoken nodded at Jake. "Fly at it!"

Jake took a lumbering step toward Trent and grinned. Trent counted three gold teeth as he put up his fist. Jake followed suit and stepped forward to take a swing at Trent and instead caught the toe of Trent's boot in his crotch. The big man let out a grunt as he bent forward, only to catch a haymaker on the side of his face. The group of men watched in astonishment as the giant fell face-first onto the ground.

The man who had urged Jake to fight shook his head. "Well, now, you sure lambasted Jake.

"Sorry, I'm a little busted from drinking last night and wasn't in the mood for a long go at it," Trent said. "When your buddy Jake wakes up, tell him I'll give him chance later if he's so minded. By the way, my brother and I are friends with the family from Boston, the Cowans, who are going with your wagon train."

"Hmm, from what I've seen of them, they'll need all the friends they can get. They know little to nothing about traveling by wagon," a short man with a ten-gallon hat said.

"You hit the nail on the head, pardner. And I reckon I'll give them all the assistance I can," Trent said.

"Yup, I believe you," another one of the group, a man with a full beard, said. "I've seen the daughter too," he said and smiled, showing blackened teeth.

Trent nodded. "Well, pardner, she ain't about to kiss that mouth of yours, that's for sure."

The man with the bad teeth laughed, and the others joined. "Well, now. I think Big Jake might have had you figured wrong. I reckon I'll give you the benefit of the doubt," he said when he stopped laughing.

"That's mighty neighborly of you. If any of you folks need help, my brother, the one who looks like our Yaqui mother, and I will be glad to help."

"Yeah, what's with that?" someone said. "You two don't look like you came out of the same mama."

"Yeah, lucky for me," Trent said and tipped his hat as he spotted Pat on the porch of the mercantile. "I've got to mosey over and join my brother."

"What, making enemies already?" Pat asked as he stared at Jake struggling to his feet.

"Nope, making friends."

Pat shook his head. "You have a funny way of making friends, Trent."

Trent glanced at the burlap bag Pat held over his shoulder. "You got the whiskey?"

"Just a bottle. The clerk said several of Mister Johnson's wagons were loaded to the top with cases of whiskey. And that being the case, I didn't see any need for us to carry more than a bottle at a time."

"So what's in the sack?"

"A pistol and gun belt for the kid. I bought him an old Colt Dragoon. If he can learn how to handle that cannon, he'll be ready for a real pistol by the time we get to Texas," Pat said.

"You've taken a shine to the kid."

"Maybe," Pat said as he stepped off the porch.

Chapter Five
The Santa Fe Trail

Trent stopped his Appaloosa at the edge of the ravine. He studied the hard-packed ground and found no signs of fresh unshod pony tracks. He reckoned the Kiowa had returned to the reservation after their encounter. Anyway, he doubted they would attack a large wagon train like Digger Johnson's.

Pat had ridden ahead to scout. Digger had warned them that a gang known as the Banditos prayed on wagons on the eastern portion of the Santa Fe Trail. He said they plied the trail between Independence and Council Grove. The leader of the gang was a Mexican man called El Asesino, the killer. He enjoyed killing and seldom left anyone alive.

The US Cavalry had failed in their attempts to apprehend the gang. In fact, they had lost several soldiers during skirmishes with the Banditos when they rode into an ambush. El Asesino had proved to be a skillful tactician and cunning as a fox, always one step ahead of the US troops.

Digger had tried to obtain an army escort to Council Grove but had been turned down. Trent figured Digger had hired him and Pat after the army refused to protect the wagon train. He didn't fear an attack by the gang. He just didn't want to be caught by surprise, which with Pat scouting ahead of the wagons wasn't likely. Pat might be only half Yaqui, but he was the best scout Trent knew.

Trent stood watching the ravine as the first wagon, one of Digger's, passed. Digger's sixteen-foot covered Murphy wagons led the caravan. Trent figured Digger thought that slower ox-drawn wagons at the rear were more likely to be attacked than the front wagons. Trent and Pat didn't like the fact that Digger cared more for the safety of his wagons than the wagons of the pioneer families. Digger Johnson was all about business.

A slight movement caught Trent's eye at the bottom of the ravine. He quickly shouldered his Sharps and set the first trigger. However, when he sighted down the barrel, he lowered his gun. He spurred his stallion lightly. The big Appaloosa slowly descended into the ravine.

At first, Trent thought the animal trapped in the snare was a Mexican gray wolf, but when he noticed the spots on its back, he realized it was more likely a mix of wolf and dog from a Kiowa camp. It had probably followed the Kiowas who had attacked the Cowans' wagon and got caught in the snare.

The dog appeared dehydrated as Trent dismounted and walked over to stand over it. Trent expected the big male dog to growl. Instead, the animal whined as it looked up at Trent. The snare had caught his right rear leg.

"You ain't going to bite me if I help you, are you?" Trent said as he knelt beside the wolf-dog. The animal whined again. "Well, now, I'm going to take that for an affirmative," Trent said as he untwisted the thin wire attached to a big rock.

It took a while. The entire time, the wolf-dog watched him in silence.

"There!" Trent exclaimed as he unwound the last of the wire from around the animal's leg. "Now go back to your master."

The wolf-dog wagged its tail.

"You're free. Get!"

The animal walked in a circle, limping slightly as the blood returned to the bad leg. Trent figured the animal would have died if he had stayed trapped another day. The wolf-dog's tongue hung out as it breathed heavily.

"You need water, I reckon," Trent said. While the wolf-dog watched, he laid his rifle against a rock and pulled his canteen from over the saddle horn. "I reckon I can spare some," Trent said and used the heel of his boot to scoop out an impression in the hard dirt. He poured it full of water and then stepped back.

Immediately, the dog walked up and lapped up the water before it could sink into the ground. When he finished, he stepped back and looked up at Trent and wagged his tail.

"Well, now, I guess you want some more," Trent said as he walked back up to the indention and poured it full of water again. "Hmm, you're a bossy one," he said as he gave the wolf-dog some distance. While the animal lapped up the water, Trent retrieved his rifle and mounted Tex. "That's all the water you're going to get from me. Now head for the mountains. I've got to get back up to the trail."

Trent urged Tex back up the bank of the ravine and didn't look back to see if the wolf-dog had run off or not. He emerged from the ravine just at Bruce walked the oxen of his second wagon past.

"Where have you been?" Bruce called out when he saw Trent ride up out of the ravine.

"I spotted a wolf-dog caught in a snare and rode down to release him," Trent replied.

"Wolfdog? I didn't know there was such a critter," Bruce said as he urged on the oxen he walked beside. "Dang it! I shouldn't have let you talk me into trading my team of horses for these oxen. They are slower than grandma." He lifted his new slouch hat and wiped the sweat from his forehead. "But ain't it dangerous to release a strange animal from a snare? You could have been bitten."

"He didn't growl, so I figured it was safe," Trent said. "Anyway, he's probably a Kiowa camp dog, and they usually aren't vicious. I'm sure he's halfway home by now."

Bruce smiled. "Ah, think again. He's following you."

Trent turned in the saddle. "Hmm, so he is. I reckon his master didn't treat him so good."

"Why would the Kiowas set traps in the ravine?" Bruce asked.

"Mexican gray wolves. They value their fur. They bait their snares with rabbit entrails. Usually, the snare catches a wolf around the neck and chokes the animal. I don't for the life of me know how this one got caught by the leg."

"What are you going to name him?" Bruce asked.

"Name him? He ain't mine."

"He's following you. That makes him yours," Bruce stated.

Trent shook his head. “No, he’ll mosey on home, I reckon, when he gets a mind to.”

Bruce chuckled. “Have it your way. But my experience is when a dog follows you home, he stays.”

“Hey, Trent.”

Trent glanced at the wagon seat in time to see Wes emerge from the inside of the wagon. “Where did you get the dog?”

“He’s a wolf-dog. I freed him from a trap in the ravine we just passed.”

“Will he bite?” Wes asked as he shared glances with the animal.

“Probably.”

“What’s his name?”

Trent said the first thing that came to his mind. “Lobo, it means wolf in Spanish.”

“Hey, Lobo. Good boy!” Wes called down to the animal. “Where are you going? Trent?”

“I’ve got to ride ahead and jaw with Pat. He’s been scouting ahead.”

“Pa, can I untie my pony from the back of the wagon and ride with Trent?” Wes asked.

“No, you can’t. And stop bothering the man. He’s got work to do,” Bruce said.

“Trent, are you and Pat eating supper with us?” Wes called after Trent.

“Nope, we eat at Digger’s mess wagon,” Trent called over his shoulder.

That was one good thing about this outfit. Digger Johnson had a mess wagon to feed all his employees. On the other wagon trains Trent had accompanied, he and Pat had been forced to scrounge up their meals by hook or by crook.

"Is that your dog?" Becky asked as Trent caught up with the Cowans' other wagon. Becky road in the seat while Lois walked alongside the oxen team. She used a long stick with a braided length of rawhide attached to the end to keep the big lumbering beasts moving.

"Your pa says he's mine," Trent said.

"Hmm, he must be yours. He looks a little mangy," Becky said before she lowered her eyes to her book.

"Are you reading about French frogs in Paris?" Trent couldn't stop himself from saying.

Becky refused to look up from her dime novel.

Trent touched his fingers to the brim of his hat as he rode ahead. He noticed Lois wore a bonnet for protection from the sun. Along with the bonnet, she wore a flowery dress and walking boots.

"Trent, I've been cussing you for miles. I hate these oxen. I must walk alongside them and switch them or else they stop. I didn't aim to walk to Texas."

"You'll have a better chance of making it to Texas with the oxen than the wagons with horses," Trent said before he urged his horse into a trot.

He didn't like that the Cowans' wagons were the last two. With their slower oxen, they and the other oxen-pulled wagons should set the pace. Already, the ten oxen-pulled wagons had dropped a quarter of a mile behind the horse-drawn wagons.

"They're bait for Kiowas and the Bandito Gang," Trent mumbled. He spurred his Appaloosa into a gallop. He wanted to jaw with Pat to let him know he planned to stay at the rear of the wagon train. He didn't want Pat straying too far ahead of the lead wagon. He wanted him to keep the wagon train in sight at all times.

Trent reined his horse up to the leading wagon when he saw Digger Johnson sitting beside the driver. "The oxen are falling too far behind," Trent called out as he slowed down his horse to match the wagon's pace.

"They can catch up when we stop for the night," Digger said in a dismissive tone.

"That means they'll more than likely arrive at the campsite after dark. That's dangerous, Digger," Trent said. He and Pat had decided to drop the "mister" when they addressed their boss. The man had hired them but had yet to earn their respect.

"Not my problem," Digger said. "Where have you been? I haven't seen you for hours."

"Back at the rear of the wagon train. If anyone is going to attack, they'll hit the rear wagons first. If they attack head on, you'll see them and have time to circle the wagons. If they charge from the rear, they won't be seen until they're right on top of the rear wagons. But then I guess you already know that," Trent said.

Digger glanced at Trent. "You do know that I'm your boss?"

"You paid me to protect the wagons. That's what I'm going to do. I'll be coming up the rear while Pat rides point," Trent said and spurred his horse into a trot before Digger could respond. The more Trent crossed paths with Digger Johnson, the less he liked the bald man. If it hadn't been for the Cowans, he would tell Pat they needed to skedaddle and find another job. However, he felt protective of the family and had a feeling that, if he and Pat departed, things wouldn't go well for the family. Trent caught up with Pat a mile ahead of the wagon train.

"Is that a wolf-dog following you?" Pat asked.

"Yup, I sprung him from a snare and now can't get rid of him," Trent said.

"He's a fine-looking animal. I guess you named him Lobo."

"How in tarnation do you know that?" Trent asked.

"He's a wolf-dog. What else would you name him?" Pat said. "Now, do you want to tell me why you rode all the way here? I'm guessing it wasn't to show off your dog."

"Digger is letting the oxen-pulled wagons fall too far behind. I'm going to stay at the rear of the wagons. I'm concerned Kiowas or bandits will hit them," Trent said.

"And I guess your hanging back has nothing to do with a pretty blond-haired, green-eyed beauty riding in one those wagons, would it?" Pat asked.

Trent winked. "Not at all, brother."

"All I can say is you are barking up the wrong tree," Pat said. "She ain't going to settle for a frontiersman, especially not one that's only half Scottish," he added with a stoic expression.

"Barking is fun too," Trent said as he turned his horse around and headed back. "And don't get out of sight of the wagons," he called over his shoulder.

Chapter Six
The Slower Wagons

Trent stood up in his stirrups. He couldn't see Digger's wagons, or the other horse-drawn wagons. Digger hadn't taken his suggestion to slow down and wait for the slower ones. He glanced up at the sun, an orange ball that hung just above the horizon. It would be full dark before they reached the other wagons.

Trent rode up and walked his horse beside Bruce Cowan. The Bostonian carried a pole similar to his wife's. He didn't use it to whip the oxen but cracked it to get their attention as he called out commands. Trent marveled at how quickly the man had learned the art of a drover. "It's going to be dark soon, Bruce. Get your oil lamp lit before it's too dark to see. I'm going to ride ahead and tell the other wagons. We can't stop until we catch them."

"Why didn't they slow down for us?" Bruce Cowan called after Trent.

Trent didn't respond as he rode up to the next wagon, only to find Jake, the giant of a man he had fought. "Hi, pardner. How are your huevos?"

The big man shook his head. "As soon as I get a chance, I'm going to wring your scrawny neck."

"Well, until that time, you should light your lantern. It's going to get dark soon. I'm guessing we have at least a mile before we catch up with the other wagons," Trent said. "Oh, and when you get ready for another licking, I'll oblige you," he tried to sound confident, but he wasn't. Yeah, his daddy had taught him to use his fist, but one blow from the big man's meat-hook sized fist would coldcock him for sure.

"A dog is following you," Jake said as Trent rode ahead.

Trent had mostly forgotten about the wolf-dog. It hadn't made a sound since he released it from the snare. At times, Lobo had wandered away, and Trent figured it had decided to return to the Kiowa camp or wherever was home. But then he would glance around and find Lobo running close on Tex's heels. "Yeah, his name is Lobo," Trent said. He again forgot about the wolf-dog as he alerted the rest of the wagons to light their lanterns. After he finished, he dropped back behind the Cowans' wagon and rode flank.

He heard a horse galloping and looked up the trail to find Pat burning leather toward him. Trent suspected his brother was exercising the big stallion, and sure enough, the first thing Pat said when he pulled the bangtail to a stop beside him was, "I bet I could make money racing him. He's as fast as the wind."

"What's happening up ahead?" Trent asked as he ignored his brother's racing comment.

"Digger has already formed a circle with the other wagons, and his cook is heating up some vittles. I thought I would ride back and see if you needed help."

"It ain't like you to miss a meal," Trent said. "And there's no helping these oxen. They move slower than snails."

"Yeah, but when those horses start dropping, the oxen will still be pulling," Pat said.

"I'm surprised Digger chose horses for his wagons."

"It's his first run. His brother has been traveling with the caravans. But he took a Comanche arrow in the leg and lost the leg from gangrene. He runs the mercantile now, and Digger oversees the wagon trains. I guess he didn't want to be slowed down by oxen."

"If that's the case, why did he allow oxen-driven wagons to join his train?" Trent asked.

Lobo whimpered.

"Something's wrong!" Trent said as he glanced down at the wolf-dog. "What is it?"

The animal looked at a low rock formation about forty yards from the trail and growled. Immediately, Trent lifted his rifle to his shoulder and scanned the rocks. The sight on the rifle always focused his eyes.

"You see anything, Pat?"

"Nope, but it's a good place for bushwhackers."

The words were just out of Pat's mouth when a dozen or so men who had forced their horses to lie down let them up and mounted.

"You called it, brother," Trent said as he pulled the trigger of his rifle. The big-bore bullet knocked one of the bandits off the back of his horse. As Trent reloaded, Pat drew and fired both pistols. Four of the attackers bit the dirt. Trent's Sharps bellowed again and blew apart the head of one of the bushwhackers. The rest of the bandits, shocked at the sudden carnage, jerked their horses around and raced away as fast as they could.

Trent glanced over at Pat. “It’s lucky you were here. I couldn’t have handled them alone.”

“Yeah, well, Digger didn’t want me to ride back to meet you. He said my job was to protect his wagons. Of course I ignored him.”

“What happened?” Bruce Cowan said when he ran up carrying his double-barrel shotgun.

“El Asesino’s men probably,” Trent said. He pointed at Pat, who had ridden out to examine the bodies. “We’ll know for sure in a while.”

“They sure caught us by surprise,” Bruce said.

“Nope, they didn’t. Lobo alerted me just before they attacked. Pat and I were ready. If we hadn’t seen them let their horses up, the outcome might have been different. We fired first and caught them by surprise instead of the other way around.”

“I guess it’s lucky you found the mutt,” Bruce said as Jake came lumbering up, carrying a Henry rifle.

“I saw it all. That was some dandy shooting, pardner,” he told Trent.

Before Trent had time to answer, Pat rode up. “I’m guessing they were members of the Bandito Gang. A couple of them were Mexican.”

“What else?” Trent asked.

“The bandits hadn’t been hiding in the grass very long. They sneaked in and took up their position behind the rocks after Digger’s wagons passed,” Pat said.

“So Digger’s refusal to wait for the oxen-drawn wagons to catch up with his wagons allowed the bushwhackers to set up the ambush,” Trent said.

"Yup," Pat agreed.

"That's interesting," Trent said. "Okay, Bruce, you and Jake get back to your wagons, and let's get going. I can see Digger's campfires. We'll be there shortly."

"Yeah, I'm bushed, Trent. Lois can hardly put one foot ahead of the other. But she is doing a game job as a drover. And the poor thing still has to whip up some vittles for supper."

Trent rode at the rear of the wagons while Pat took the lead. Trent looked down. Lobo trotted beside Tex, looking more wolf than dog. Trent had begun to suspect Lobo had belonged to a trapper and not to Kiowas. Maybe the Banditos had killed his master, and that was why he had alerted Trent to the presence of the gang. Whatever the reason, he was glad to have struck up a friendship with the big wolf-dog.

Trent turned his thoughts to Digger Johnson. The man's disregard for the safety of the Cowan family and the other wagons drawn by oxen puzzled him. Sure, they had a different reason for taking to the Santa Fe Trail than Digger Johnson. His purpose was to make a profit selling the supplies he carried on his wagons. The others were seeking a new life in the West. Still, the safety of all the wagons fell on the shoulders of the wagon master. It was brewing in Trent's mind that, maybe when they reached Council Grove, he'd advise Bruce Cowan to hook up with a different wagon train. Council Grove was also a collection point for wagons headed farther west on the Santa Fe Trail.

Pat's arrival interrupted Trent's thoughts. He pulled Leo alongside Tex. "Digger didn't leave an opening for the other wagons."

Trent shook his head. "I don't know what his game is, Pat. I guess we better have these wagons form a second circle. Ride up to the lead wagon and help them circle the wagons. I'll keep guard on the rear. We might not have seen the last of the Bandito Gang."

"Ah, you just want to stay close to the gal," Pat accused before he raced off on his spirited mustang.

It took another hour for the wagons to get aligned in a circle. Trent heard men and women yelling gee and haw often. He knew from traveling with other wagon trains that oxen were smart. They not only obeyed whip signals and hand signals but watched the drover to anticipate which way he wanted them to walk. The Cowans' oxen teams were Red Durhams and weighed over a ton each. He had noticed Devon oxen pulling other wagons. They were slightly smaller than Red Durhams. It took the drovers additional time to unyoke the oxen and loosen them in the center of the circled wagons. Trent and Pat stayed with the wagon train until the settlers finished with the wagons and oxen.

"You boys stay and share vittles with us," Bruce said. He motioned over to where Lois and Becky worked over a campfire, making flapjacks and frying bacon. "And I would feel safer if you would bunk down under our wagons."

Trent glanced over at Pat. "Thanks, I'm sure your wife's cooking is better than the tobacco-chewing old coot Digger hired for a cook. Pat will keep you company while I mosey over and jaw with Digger."

Trent felt Becky's eyes on him as he walked out of the circle of wagons to where he had Tex tied to a wagon wheel. He smiled to himself. If she was looking, she was interested. Before he rode over to the other wagons, he made a full circle around the area where the families with oxen had made camp. He watched Lobo to see how he reacted. He didn't show any signs of alarm, so Trent finally headed to Digger's camp.

"Who goes there?" someone yelled from behind one of the wagons as Trent approached.

"Trent!"

"Okay," came the reply.

Trent noticed Lobo stayed beside Tex when he tied the Appaloosa to the nearest wagon wheel and stepped over the wagon tongue and into the camp. A slew of men in red plaid shirts sat around a campfire, over which a huge pot hung from an iron tripod.

"Where have you been, Trent?" Digger called out from a chair near the fire.

"Helping the wagons you left on their own. They were ambushed a ways back," Trent said.

Digger nodded. "I heard the shots."

Trent waited for the man to continue, but Digger fell silent. "You don't seem too concerned," Trent threw the statement at the man like an accusation.

Digger shrugged. "They chose oxen. They could have bought horses or mules."

"Some families couldn't afford either. If you weren't going to match the pace set by the oxen, why let them join the wagon train?" Trent asked.

"I had my reasons. Now I think it's time you remember who you and your brother work for, and it's not the Cowan family or any other of the pilgrims."

"Well, Digger, let me put it this way. If you don't slow down and match the pace of the slower wagons, Pat and I will stay behind to protect them. You can go ahead on your own."

"You won't get paid," Digger said.

"Yup, I know, but what I said still goes. And the Banditos might want to exact revenge for the gang members Pat and I put in the dirt. If they do, I figure they'll be more inclined to hit the larger wagon train that's not protected by my Sharps and Pat's Colts."

"You and your brother are high on your self worth."

"We know our value to a wagon train of clerks. We've been traveling with wagon trains since both our parents were killed by Apaches three years ago. There ain't much we don't know about the dangers of the trail."

Digger didn't respond.

"You'll be going through Apache and Comanche territory, both of which are on the warpath these days. They're far more dangerous than the Bandito Gang," Trent continued. "Your clerks can't handle an attack by either tribe."

Digger sighed, and then reluctantly nodded. "Okay, I'll match their pace. However, I'm cutting you and your brother's pay in half."

"Fine. It ain't about the money with Pat and me," Trent said.

"Nah, with you, it's about the Cowans' girl. I saw how you looked at her in the store. You gave her the puppy dog eyes."

"Digger, be careful what you say next," Trent said in an icy tone.

Digger cleared his throat. "If there is nothing else, you can go now."

Trent touched the brim of his hat before he turned on his heels and walked away.

"I saw a wolf beside your horse. When I raised my rifle to shoot him, he vanished," the guard said as Trent approached him.

Trent swung the barrel of his rifle from the crook of his arm and stuck the muzzle under the man's chin. "You shoot my dog, and you might as well shoot yourself!"

The man's eyes bulged. "I... I didn't know it was your dog. It looked like a wolf!" he protested.

Trent put his gun away. "Now you know. Pass the word. Kill Trent's dog, kill yourself!"

"Yes, sir, Mister Trent. I'll do that!"

Trent smiled. "Thanks." He stepped over the wagon tongue and mounted Tex. He had barely left the vicinity of the wagons before Lobo joined him. Trent glanced down. "So you've been shot at before. Well, so have I."

"Vittles are ready. Chow down!" Bruce called out when Trent walked up to the campfire.

"Trent, the two women know how to fix grub," Pat said as he took a bite of a flapjack and washed it down with a tin cup of coffee.

Lois, who sat beside Bruce, nodded over at Becky, who sat with Wes. "My daughter made the flapjacks."

Trent lifted one off the tin plate resting on a barrel near the fire. "I didn't know they taught you how to make flapjacks in a dime novel," he said as he walked past Becky on his way to join Pat.

"I guess you'll never know since I doubt you can read," Becky said.

Trent sat cross-legged on the ground next to Pat. "My father made me read the works of Shakespeare when I was twelve," Trent said and winked.

Chapter Seven
El Asesino

Trent decided to bed down under the wagon where Bruce's family slept while Pat slept across the circle of wagons under another wagon. Still leery of an attack by the leader of the Banditos, Trent wanted both sides of the wagons covered. El Asesino had lost several of his men and probably wouldn't take that lying down. Now, instead of looking for a profit, he would be out for blood first and loot second.

And heavens knew the pioneers would be easy targets. Some carried Winchester rifles, but most were like Bruce Cowan and had only a shotgun for hunting. Trent doubted the men had more than a couple of pistols to their names.

Digger's men were better armed, but for the most part, they were clerks and not frontiersmen. Trent doubted any of them could shoot straight. They were more than likely to flee across the prairie at the first sounds of gunshots.

Trent figured Digger had been counting on the army escort. When they pulled out of the assignment at the last moment, the man had no choice but to hire Trent and his brother as escorts. He had begun to think he and Pat had made a mistake accepting work from Digger. As far as he was concerned, there was something dishonest about the man.

Trent decided to take a stroll around the perimeter before calling it a night. He already had his bedroll and saddle laid out under the wagon. The bed called to Trent as he walked around the wagons. It was late, and he would be up before sunrise.

As he walked, he realized he had a shadow. He glanced back. Lobo, looking entirely like a wolf, matched his pace. "Looks like you've bonded with me." The wolf-dog didn't show any signs he heard Trent. He seemed more interested in the night scents. He kept testing the slight breeze as though on the scent of something. However, he didn't shown any signs of alarm, so Trent figured all was well.

"You still up, Trent?" Pat called out as Trent walked by the wagon under which he had chosen to bunk.

"Making one last round. All's quiet so far. Can't hear anything but crickets and frogs. Lobo hasn't picked up an alarming scent. So I guess we're good for the moment."

"Yeah, for the moment," Pat repeated his words. "But I can't see this El Asesino being a forgiving soul."

"Yup, my sentiments exactly. If nothing else, he has a reputation to uphold," Trent said. "So sleep with one eye open, brother," Trent said as he continued his rounds. By the time he crawled under the Cowans' wagon, Trent's eyelids wouldn't stay open. A moment after he rested his head against his saddle, sleep overcame him. He didn't feel the big furry body snuggle up against him like a puppy against his mother.

Vibrations.

Lobo growled and sprung to his feet as Trent opened his eyes.

Horses. Lots of horses!

"An attack!" Trent shouted as he crawled out from under the wagon, holding his Sharps. He glanced across the prairie. At least forty mounted men brandishing rifles charged the wagons.

"What?" Bruce said as he stuck his head out of the front of the wagon.

"Bandits! Get your scattergun and tell everyone in the wagon to hunker down!" Trent yelled as he lifted his rifle to his shoulder. The horsemen might be out of range, but the blast of the .50 caliber Sharps would wake the entire wagon train, even if he missed his shot.

This time, Trent took a moment to aim. The shot was impossible, but Trent pulled the trigger just the same.

"You put one in the dirt," Bruce said when he joined Trent.

"Lucky shot," Trent said as he reloaded. "Get behind the wagon wheel. It's not much protection, but some." Trent fired again. "Now that wasn't a lucky shot," he said as another of the riders fell off his horse.

"I don't hear any shooting from Digger's wagons," Bruce said.

"Strange," Trent commented before he squeezed the trigger a third time. Another rider pitched backward off his horse.

Men in the wagons on both ends of Bruce's wagon opened fire with Winchesters. However, they missed their targets. As Trent pulled his pistol, Pat slid under the wagon, flipped over on his belly, and drew his guns.

He winked at Trent. "I bet I get more."

"I'm three ahead already," Trent replied before both opened fire.

The rapid pistol shots sounded like a Gatling gun. Riders fell off their horses like falling dominoes. Yet still they charged, with a big mustachioed Mexican man shouting at them to kill everyone.

Bruce fired first one barrel of his scattergun and then the other, taking two more outlaws out of the fray. Bullets kicked up dirt all around the wagon. Trent felt a sharp pain in his left upper arm. He ignored it as he reloaded his pistol. Pat beat him reloading. He fired point-blank as several attackers swerved their mounts to avoid colliding with the wagon. Five fell off their horses. Bruce's shotgun roared again, making a mess of one of the outlaws. Then the attackers swept around the wagons, yelling and shooting into the covered wagons.

Trent heard a man yell in pain from inside one of the wagons. A woman screamed in another. Trent glanced over at Digger's wagons. Silence. Not one rifle fired at the attackers. He made a note to himself that, if he lived through the attack, he would make that man pay. It had become evident to him the oxen wagons were the sacrificial lambs to appease El Asesino.

"Trent, I'm going to get the leader," Pat said as he finished loading his pistols.

"No, no," Bruce said. "You can't leave the wagons. You'll get shot." He spoke to Pat's back because the wiry man had darted out from under the wagon and sprinted toward the circling attackers.

His action took the attackers by surprise. He had closed the distance by half before they fired. Trent picked off the rider nearest his brother. Pat matched pace with the riderless horse and managed to grab the saddle horn. In a blink of an eye, he vaulted into the saddle. Then Pat bent over the side of the horse and shot from under the horse's neck. He killed four outlaws before spotting the leader.

Pat steered the horse in pursuit of El Asesino. The big Mexican man spotted Pat and broke off from the circling riders and made a mad dash for the open prairie. Pat spoiled that option. He shot the outlaw's horse out from under him.

El Asesino hit the ground mustache first and took in a mouthful of grass and dirt. He tried to get up and run as Pat bore down on him. But the man's legs gave way. He fell. He shot but Pat returned fire and shot him while he lay sprawled on the ground.

Trent took that moment to put another of the attackers in the dirt. Seeing their leader dead and losing another member of the gang broke the bandits' spirit. As one, they turned their horses and raced for the open prairie.

As Pat dismounted, he asked, "Trent, how's the shoulder?"

"Luckily hit the left. I can get along with a bum arm," Trent said. When he saw Becky stick her head out of the wagon, he nodded at her. "How are your mother and brother?"

"Fine. We lay down in the bed of the wagon during the shooting. Going to have to pick lead out of the barrels of cornmeal and flour though," Becky said.

"Pa, is my pony all right?" Wes asked as he joined his sister on the wagon seat.

"Yup," Trent answered.

"You're bleeding!" Becky exclaimed when she noticed blood on Trent's left sleeve.

"Just a scratch," Trent replied.

"Did someone get shot?" Lois said as she made her way out of the back of the wagon.

"Trent got hit in the shoulder," Becky said, sounding concerned.

Lois climbed off the wagon. "Come over here and let me have a look at it."

Trent didn't move.

"We can't afford your wound to get infected. Let my wife clean and bandage your shoulder," Bruce said.

"Where's that big dog of yours?" Lois asked.

"He ripped the throat out of one of the bandits who tried to climb into my wagon to get to my wife and two girls," Ralf said as he walked up with Lobo at his side. "He sure doesn't like those men."

"I think the Banditos might have killed his owner," Trent said as Lois cut open the sleeve of his buckskin shirt to look at the wound. "Ah, this is the only shirt I own," he added.

Becky wrinkled her nose. "Yep, I can tell."

Trent looked wounded.

"He can have one of my shirts," Bruce said.

Trent nodded. "As long as it's not red plaid," he added as Lobo walked up and sniffed his hand.

"He won't bite me, will he?" Lois asked as she glanced down at the big wolf-dog.

"Probably not as long as you don't hurt me," Trent said as he winced when Lois dabbed a wet cloth over the shallow groove the bullet had gouged out of his arm at the shoulder joint.

"Trent McLeod, for heavens sakes, you are a baby to make such a face when Ma cleans your scratch," Becky accused.

"He never could stand the sight of his own blood," Pat said.

"Don't you have chores to do?" Trent said. "Go and see who else got shot. I heard a couple of screams during the shooting," he added.

"Yeah, I better. Just don't go and faint on them," Pat added before he turned and walked away.

"I never know when he's serious or joking," Bruce said. "His facial expression never changes."

Lois stepped back from Trent. "Okay, I'm finished. You'll live to fight another day." She turned back to the wagon. "Becky, come and fetch Trent one of your pa's shirts."

"Trent," Bruce said softly once both of the women were in the wagon."I think I saw Mathias Coruthers in Independence."

Trent looked puzzled.

"He's the reason we fled Boston. He's the head of the gang who runs the Boston shipyards. He was going to force Becky to marry him. Lois and I couldn't let that happen. Mathias is an ugly brute of a man. Becky would have been treated worse than a slave."

Trent came to full attention.

"He had several of his gang members with him. They're Irish thugs that, like him, enjoy killing. I'm concerned about Becky's safety. I don't doubt he plans on abducting her if he catches up with us."

"This Mathias fellow must have some strong feelings for your daughter to travel all the way from Boston," Trent said.

"Well, I suspect he plans on killing me. I tricked him into thinking I approved of his marriage to Becky. He must've been fit to be tied when he learned we fled Boston."

Trent shook his head. "As long as I can shoot, nobody's going to lay a hand on your daughter, Bruce."

Bruce nodded. "That's reassuring. Thanks."

"Pa, is this shirt all right for Trent?" Becky asked as she jumped down from the wagon.

Bruce glanced at the tan-colored shirt and nodded. "It goes with his tan hat."

Becky tossed the shirt to Trent. "Here, take off that mangy buckskin shirt and burn it."

"Becky…" Bruce called out.

"Well, Pa, it stinks."

"You can't wash buckskin. It's liable to shrink too much. You have to freeze it. I can't do that in the spring," Trent protested.

Becky rolled her eyes. "I think Pa can spare one of his shirts for Pat, too. Tell him to burn his too. I don't want to smell stinking buckskin all the way to California."

"Becky, we might not go to California," Bruce said. "You know I have my heart set on a piece of land in Texas."

"Well, Pa, I've got my heart set on finding a nice rich man in California to marry," Becky said. She looked at Trent while she spoke.

Chapter Eight
Life on the Trail

Pat shook his head. "I'm not burning my shirt."

"Yes, you are if you want to spend time around the Cowans. I know you like Wes and are secretly teaching him to shoot despite his father forbidding him to handle a pistol."

Pat shook his head. "You wouldn't tell Bruce?"

"Oh, yes, I would. Becky wants you to burn your buckskin shirt, and you're going to burn it," Trent said.

"She's got you wrapped around her pinky, and she's set on marrying some rich Californian," Pat said.

"It's a long way to California. And women change their minds more often than a pony express rider changes horses," Trent said. He tossed a red shirt to Pat. "Burn the buckskin shirt and put this on."

"What are we going to do about Digger?" Pat asked, changing the subject as they watched the wagons break up their circle and head on the trail. He had worked with Jessie Beckett to get her two teams of oxen yoked and hooked to the wagon. He had felt sorry for the pretty redhead. Luckily, she had helped her husband handle the oxen and knew what to do on the trail.

"And don't think I didn't see you helping Widow Beckett with her oxen. And her husband barely cold in the ground," Trent said.

Pat didn't respond.

Trent shifted his rifle from the crook of his arm. "Darn, my shoulder aches something fierce." He glanced up the trail where the larger wagon train had also gotten underway. "I guess it's time we ended our employment with Digger. I can't abide by a man who would sit back and watch men and women killed without lifting a finger."

"How many of the settlers did the outlaws kill?" Pat asked.

"Five, and three of them were children. Sam Beckett took a bullet in the chest. Now his wife, Jessie, must take over as drover, but you already know that. Martin Sawyer's wife got hit in the head, and their baby is dead, too. Ralf Reynolds' two daughters were shot dead. His wife won't stop bawling. I sure feel sorry for them."

"It could have been worse," Pat said.

Trent nodded. "And it would have if you hadn't killed El Asensio."

He walked over to Tex. Lobo, who had been lying in the grass a few feet away, sprung to his feet.

"Where are you heading?" Pat asked.

"I think it's time we moseyed on up and had a heart-to-heart talk with Digger Johnson," Trent said.

Trent struggled to mount the Appaloosa with his bad arm. He noticed today Digger seemed to keep the pace more in tune with what the oxen could maintain. Still, he fumed silently as he approached the lead wagon.

Digger sat beside the driver, reading a newspaper. Upon hearing Trent's and Pat's horses, he glanced over.

"Were you reading the newspaper this morning during the attack?" Trent asked. "'Cause you sure didn't make any attempt to help us out and repel the outlaws."

Digger laid the newspaper on the seat beside him. "What could I do? Your wagons were too far away for my men to join in the fray. We might have killed some settlers instead of the outlaws. Anyway, they're clerks to help me sell my goods on the trail and not frontiersmen. My wagons are rolling mercantile stores."

"Okay, Digger, this is what you're going to do. Make sure you keep matching the oxen's pace. And at the end of the day, all the wagons, horse and oxen-drawn are going to form one big circle, with the oxen and horses in the middle to graze."

"Now, wait a minute. I'm the wagon master and not you, Trent. You can't go giving me orders!"

"My brother killed El Asesino during the attack. He wants to do the same to you for not helping defend the wagons, but I told him we would give you one more chance to do what's right by the settlers."

"You can't threaten Mister Digger," Doug, the driver, said and grabbed for his iron, which flew out of his hand as Pat drew and fired his right pistol.

"Ouch!" Doug said, grabbing his injured hand.

Pat twirled his pistol back into his holster. "Try that again, and I'll put a blue whistler between those dumb eyes of yours."

Two riders galloped up with pistols drawn.

"Tell your men to holster their guns, or I'll kill them both," Pat warned.

Digger, who had turned a shade paler as he took Pat's warning to heart, shouted. "Put away your guns! Get back to your positions. Those four whiskey wagons are worth more than ten of the other wagons."

"Whiskey?" Trent said.

"Yeah, for trade. Whiskey is worth its weight in gold in these frontier towns," Digger explained.

"Digger, I don't intend to jaw all day with you," Trent said. "I hope you understand my position because, should I have to confront you again, I'm afraid you're going to be missing some body parts!"

"Just so you two know, I'm not paying you a dime! Both of you are fired!" Digger said.

"That sits well with my brother and me," Trent said. "We don't cotton to working for a cheat."

Digger swallowed the words he wanted to say and remained silent.

Trent turned in the saddle. "Pat, scout ahead. We're moving into Comanche territory. They might not be as fierce as the Kiowa, but they aren't friendly, and they're practically born on horses. No one fights better from horseback than a Comanche."

"Except for a Yaqui," Pat said before galloping off.

"I guess I'll mosey back to the rear," he started to rein Tex around but stopped. "Digger, you pull another fast one, and you'll never hear my rifle shot. Do you catch my drift?"

The man didn't answer.

Trent tipped his hat and spun his Appaloosa around. He heard Digger mumble something as he trotted away. He paused when he reached Ralf walking alongside his lead team of oxen. "Sorry about your daughters."

"Thanks. I can live with it since I know that Mexican devil is gone. I hope he's burning in hell," the big man said. "Thank your brother for me. Tell him I owe him one."

"Sure," Trent said, not knowing what else to say. As he rode away, his thoughts turned back to the moment he and Pat had returned from town to find their two wagons burning and the mutilated bodies of their parents sprawled on the ground like dismembered rag dolls. The handy work of Apaches.

The war party of ten Apaches had not lived long to celebrate taking Juanita and Roger McLeod's lives. Trent had laid on a bluff overlooking their camp and shot eight of them, one at a time. Pat gunned down the two who hightailed it in the opposite direction. Still, it had taken weeks for the pain in his chest to become bearable.

"Trent," Wes called out as he rode up on his pony. "Where's Pat? We... we were going for a ride."

"You mean he was going to continue your pistol lessons," Trent said.

"You know?"

"Yup," Trent said.

"Don't tell my pa. He's dead set against me learning to draw a pistol," Wes said.

"Na, I'll keep your secret." Trent lifted his hat and ran his fingers through his blond hair. "Ah, does your sister ever talk about me?"

"She says you are an uncivilized cowboy," Wes said.

Trent's face dropped.

Wes chuckled when he saw Trent's reaction. "But she likes you. Becky just won't admit it. She's still got it in her head that some rich man in California is going to beg to marry her. All the girls in the dime novels she reads marry well-to-do men."

Suddenly Wes's pony neighed and reared up. Wes slipped off the back of the pony while the animal pawed the air with his front legs. When the pony's hooves touched the ground, it sidestepped a rattlesnake curled to strike again.

Trent drew his pistol and fired. His bullet hit the snake in the head and knocked it a few feet. "Wes," Trent called as he vaulted from Tex and ran over to the boy.

"What happened?" Wes asked as he sat up.

"A rattlesnake," Trent said as he helped the boy to his feet.

"Look!" Wes yelled and pointed at his pony. The spotted pony held his right front leg off the ground. "The snake bit him."

Trent walked over and leaned over to examine the pony's leg. "Yup, the snake got him good. Sorry, Wes."

"What do you mean? My pony will be okay, won't he? Tell me he'll be okay," Wes said with desperation in his voice.

Trent shook his head. "That snake is almost eight feet long. One that big carries a lot of poison. Your pony won't last the night," Trent said as he grabbed hold of the pony's reins. "I'll take him out and shoot him. If I don't, he'll die a horrible death."

"No, no! You can't shoot my pony! You can't!"

"What's the matter?" Bruce shouted as he ran up to them, breathing heavily.

"Trent is going to shoot my pony, Pa. Don't let him."

Bruce glanced at Trent. Trent pointed over at the dead rattlesnake. "He bit the pony. Ain't nothing I can do but put him out of his misery, else the pony is going to feel a heap of pain before he dies."

Bruce took a deep breath. He turned to face his son. "Wes, Trent is right. The pony will die. Let's give him a merciful death."

"But, Pa, can't you do something to save him?"

Bruce shook his head. "Hug him and then walk back to the wagon with me. Be brave, Wes."

Wes glanced at Trent.

"It'll be quick. The pony won't feel any pain, Wes. I promise. And I'll get you another one, I promise," Trent said.

"You promise?" Wes asked.

Trent nodded his head.

"Go over and give him a hug," Bruce repeated.

Wes sighed. He nodded, and then slowly walked over to the pony. The boy sobbed as he grabbed the pony around the neck. Then he let go, turned, and walked over to his father.

"Come along, Wes. You can help me with the oxen," Bruce said.

Trent felt sorry for Wes as he got back on his horse. He hated putting the pony down but knew it was the best thing to do. As he headed back to the wagons, Trent spotted Pat burning leather toward him. He hoped his brother was riding back to check on the gunshot. He pulled Tex up and waited for Pat.

"I guess you rode back to investigate my shot?"

Pat shook his head. "No, I spotted a group of Comanche hunters up ahead. They're butchering several buffalo they shot. Since they have their women along, I don't expect trouble. What should we do? Wait until they are finished or proceed?"

"Did you tell Digger?" Trent asked.

"No, it's our decision. I don't trust him."

Trent nodded. "Neither do I."

"What did you shoot? A rabbit?" Pat asked.

"No, I had to put Wes's pony down. A rattlesnake bit him. The boy is upset." Trent shrugged. "I promised him a new pony."

"The Comanches have extra horses," Pat said.

"Yeah, maybe we can trade for one?" Trent said. "Bruce certainly has enough supplies. He brought tools to build a log cabin and God knows what else."

"So should we keep the wagons moving?" Pat asked.

Trent shook his head. "No, we stop the wagon train for the day and give the Comanche time to finish up butchering the buffaloes they killed. They might not be a war party, but one of Digger's men might do something foolish to set them off."

"You want me to tell Digger?" Pat asked.

"No, you ride over to Bruce and ask him what's he willing to trade the Comanche for a horse for Wes. Then you ride ahead and trade with the Comanches. You look Yaqui. You tell them you're a scout for a well-armed wagon train." Trent took a deep breath. "I'll deal with Digger."

Pat wheeled Leo around.

"Pat, trade for two horses. One for Wes and one for Becky. I want to teach her how to ride."

"That's downright devious, brother," Pat said before kneeing his mustang into a gallop.

"Yup, it is," Trent said as he rode toward the front of the wagon train.

Chapter Nine
Bad Weather

Digger Johnson glanced over when Trent's Appaloosa matched pace with his wagon. His face registered displeasure at the sight of the young blond frontiersman and the dog trailing him. He waited for Trent to speak first.

"Pat discovered a group of Comanches hunting buffalo up ahead. We've decided to stop the wagons until they finish dressing their kills. What you do is up to you."

Digger shook his head. "Well, I ain't stopping for a hunting party of Comanches. They ain't going to attack us with women and children among them."

"Suit yourself. However, I advise against continuing until tomorrow."

"I need to get my wagons of trade goods in the hand of merchants before someone else beats me to it. Time is money for me. I ain't looking for a spot of dirt to lay claim to like your settlers."

"Pat is going to try trading with them. We need horses. I'll have him stop by and let you know the mood of the group," Trent said before he wheeled Tex around and galloped back in the direction of the slower wagons. As he approached, he noted Pat and Bruce were already directing the drovers to circle the wagons.

"Let me guess," Pat called out as Trent approached. "Digger isn't going to stop."

"You hit the nail on the head. But it's his wagons and his scalp to lose," Trent replied. "But we both know the Comanches are a cunning bunch. The hunting party might just be a ploy to lure the wagons into an ambush," Trent said.

"I'll check things out between here and the hunting party. If I see signs of an ambush, I'll race lickety-split back," Pat said.

"What do you have to trade?"

"Bruce gave me some hatchets and a couple of bottles of whiskey."

"What's Bruce doing with extra whiskey?"

"For trade. He found out Digger had packed several wagons with whiskey and decided he would do the same. Whiskey is lighter than hammers, anvils, and such. He figures he can trade whiskey for the tools he needs to build his log cabin. Maybe even trade some for logs."

"That's fine, but I do hate giving Comanches whiskey. It could put them in a killing mood. But I want those two horses," Trent admitted.

"And we both know why," Pat said before he gave his mustang his head and galloped away.

"Why are we stopping?" Becky called out as Trent passed her wagon.

"Hunting party of Comanches up ahead."

Becky stood up in the wagon and shaded her eyes with her hand. “I don’t see them.”

“They’re over the horizon. We’re going to hold up here until tomorrow to make sure it’s safe,” Trent explained.

“But the other wagons aren’t stopping?”

Trent shrugged. “Digger decided to continue.”

“You don’t like Mister Johnson, do you, Trent?” Becky said.

“No, he’s a scoundrel.”

“But you and your brother work for him?” Becky said in a puzzled tone.

Trent shook his head. “Not anymore. Oh, later today, I might have a surprise for you.”

Becky’s eyes lit up. “For me?”

Trent smiled at her reaction. “Yes, for you.”

“What is it? Tell me. I hate surprises. But it better not be a big ugly dog like Lobo.”

Trent shook his head. “No, you’ll have to wait.” Trent glanced to the right. “Those clouds gathering are plenty black. I think we might be in for a storm. I better go speak to your father about the change in the weather.” He started to turn Tex around but stopped. “Once the wagons are circled, you and your mother best get under the wagons.”

“Why?” Becky asked.

“Just do it!” Trent snapped as he spotted three funnel-shaped clouds drop down from a huge dark thunderhead. Tornados! And they were heading toward the wagons. Trent rode over to Bruce’s other wagon. He interrupted Bruce and Lois as they removed the yokes from the two teams of oxen.

Trent pointed at the funnel clouds in the distance. "Tornadoes! They're heading this way."

"Tornadoes?" Bruce questioned. "Are they bad? We don't have tornadoes in Boston. But I've heard of them."

"They can lift a log cabin up into the sky. Is that bad enough for you?"

"I reckon so. What do we do?"

"Get the oxen unyoked and in the center of the wagons. Then lie under the wagon and not inside. You'll have a better chance of surviving if one of the funnel clouds hits. They'll rip the wagons apart. You don't want to be inside of one that gets caught up in a twister," Trent explained.

As the settlers worked feverously to unyoke their oxen, the funnel clouds moved closer. The sky darkened like it was almost night as Trent directed the settlers to get under their wagons. The wind picked up. It started to rain. Underneath, the wagons provided little protection from the wind-blown rain. However, Trent wouldn't allow the settlers back into the wagons.

Digger's wagons had disappeared over the horizon. From the direction the funnel clouds were traveling, Trent figured the wagons and the hunting party of Comanches were safe. He wished the same was true for the settlers' wagons. The funnel clouds lifted into the clouds, only to descend again a few moments later.

Trent, having done all he could to prepare the wagons for a possible hit by a tornado, crawled under the wagon with Bruce and his family. They had wrapped themselves with horse blankets against the rain. Seeing Trent, Bruce offered him a blanket.

While the wind whipped sheets of rain under the wagon, Trent wrapped himself with only his head sticking out. Lobo lay at his side, curled up in a ball. Trent stuffed his hat in his lap under the blanket. He glanced at Becky. Her blanket completely covered her from head to foot, the same for Lois and Wes. Like Trent, Bruce had his head exposed.

"Doggone it!" Trent yelled. One of the funnel clouds touched down and was headed straight for the wagons.

Bruce moaned in fear at the sight of the destruction the twisting winds of the tornado caused as it moved rapidly across the prairie. It uprooted trees and sucked them up into its dark funnel while it grew nearer and nearer to the wagons.

"Lie down! It's going to hit!" Trent yelled as he reached over and pushed Becky to the ground.

It sounded like a train. Trent looked death in the eye as the tornado struck a wagon on the opposite side of the circle. He watched in horror as the twisting winds lifted the sixteen-foot Murphy wagon and spun it like a top.

We are next, Trent thought as he watched the funnel cloud lift an ox from the center of the wagons on its way toward the Cowans' wagon. He forced himself not to close his eyes. He would look death in the face.

A moment before it touched the wagon, the funnel lifted. It passed over the wagon, sounding like a train. Trent heard a crash. The wagon that had been sucked up into the tornado dropped less than ten feet from where he and the Cowan family sheltered under their wagon. The wagon splintered into kindling wood, spewing barrels of flour and cornmeal onto the ground along with an assortment of tools. A dead ox lay beyond the wagon.

Suddenly the sun peeked out from behind the clouds.

"It's over," Trent declared as he threw the blanket off and crawled out from under the wagon. He put on his hat as he raced into the middle of the circle formed by the wagons in search of Tex. The Appaloosa stallion spotted him first and neighed. Trent hurried over to the horse and patted him on the forehead as he looked around at the wagons.

A young couple, Marty and Grace Jones, sat up and looked around, dazed to find their wagon gone. "It landed over beyond the Cowans' wagon," Trent said as he led Tex over to the couple. "You're darn lucky the tornado didn't suck the both of you up with the wagon."

Grace buried her face in her hands and sobbed. She ignored Lobo as the big dog walked up and sniffed her.

Marty nodded at Trent. "Everything we owned was in the wagon. Now we got nothing."

"You have your lives! Everything else can be replaced. Come on over to the Cowans' wagon. You can travel in their second one. They could use another drover, Marty." Trent said. "And I spotted some of your belongings scattered around the ruins of your wagon. You might salvage some things.

"One of our oxen is missing. We only had one team," Marty explained as he helped his wife to her feet.

Trent counted the wagon train very lucky as he walked around the circle. The tornado had destroyed only the wagon belonging to the Joneses and killed one of their oxen.

It could have easily destroyed the entire wagon train and killed everyone.

"How is it possible the clouds are gone!" Becky said as she and her mother walked over to join Trent.

Trent shook his head. "Look, a rainbow." He pointed across the prairie.

"It's beautiful. God's promise of better things to come," Lois said.

"Miss Lois, I told the Joneses they could ride in your second wagon, and maybe he could be the drover for the wagon. I hope that's all right with you and Bruce?" Trent said.

"Yes, yes, I am tired of playing drover. I guess there's a silver lining in every dark cloud," Lois said. "I see Marty and Grace over at the wagon. I'll go over and talk to them."

"So where's the surprise you promised me?" Becky asked once they were alone.

Trent glanced up the trail. "Go get Wes. I have a surprise for him too," Trent said.

Becky shrugged. "Okay."

Trent looked up the trail again. Pat approached at a gallop, leading two horses. Good, he had worried the Comanches wouldn't trade. He stood patting Tex on the forehead as he waited for Pat to arrive. Trent shook his head. "Those don't look like Comanche ponies."

"Nope, one is a young Morgan mare and the other a red roan quarter horse gelding," Pat said.

"I'm not going to ask what probably happened to their original owners," Trent said.

"Dead, for sure." Pat offered.

"Please don't tell Becky or Wes. It's better if they think both are Comanche horses," Trent said. He spotted Becky and Wes heading their way. "They're coming."

Pat dismounted. "The Morgan is very gentle. She'll make a good match for Becky. The red roan is a cutting horse. He has plenty of cow sense. He'll outrun either of our mounts for a short distance. He's a first-rate piece of horseflesh."

"What have you got, Pat?" Wes asked. His eyes lit up when he spotted the two horses. He turned to Trent. "Is one of them for me?"

Trent nodded. "Yes, I told you I would get you another horse."

"I hope it's the big red roan?" Wes said. He walked up to the Quarter Horse and patted him on the forehead.

"Yes," Trent said. "Here, let me help you up."

"Without a saddle?" Wes asked.

"Yeah, Pat will walk him around with you on his back. You'll be all right," Trent said as he interlaced his fingers to let Wes use his hands as a stirrup. "There, how does it feel to be on him?"

"Great, he's so much bigger than my pony," Wes said as Pat led the Quarter Horse away.

Trent nodded at Becky. "The Morgan mare is yours."

"I don't know how to ride," Becky said.

Trent smiled. "I'll teach you. Then you won't have to ride on the wagon all day."

"That would be nice. And when we pass close to a town, I could ride over and do some shopping," Becky said as her voice turned eager. "But I'll need a nice saddle."

"Your father has a couple of saddles in the second wagon he brought along to trade."

"Yeah, the second wagon is almost all trade goods. Pa put almost all his money in items he thought would fetch him a good profit farther west," Becky said.

"Good, I'll start giving you riding lessons tomorrow," Trent said with an ear-to-ear smile.

Chapter Ten
Comanches!

Breakfast before first light had been pleasant. Becky was friendly and eager to learn how to ride the black Morgan mare. Wes bubbled over with enthusiasm over his Quarter Horse. He had named the horse Major. And sure enough, Bruce had produced two saddles from the second wagon where Marty and Grace rode and slept now. Marty drove the oxen, to Lois's relief.

However, when the sun emerged as a red ball from below the horizon, Trent glanced up the trail. A chill went down his spine. Smoke, thick black smoke curled up from below the horizon up the trail. "Pat," Trent shouted. "Look!"

"The Comanches attacked Digger Johnson's wagons!" Pat said.

Trent nodded. "Burned them!"

"What about Digger Johnson and his men?" Bruce asked.

Pat answered. "Dead, probably."

"We need to go and help them," Bruce said.

"No, keep the wagons circled. They might attack us," Trent said.

"But we have to go and see if anyone is alive," Bruce insisted.

"Pat and I'll go. You and the others arm yourselves and prepare for an attack. However, the Comanches probably don't think the rest worthwhile since you don't have horses. They aren't going to risk getting shot to steal oxen."

"How's your shoulder?" Bruce asked. "Can you load your rifle?"

Trent shrugged. "I might be a shade slower, that's all. It doesn't affect my aim."

Pat rode up, leading Tex. "Let's go and kill some Comanches."

Becky shook her head. "I hate frontiersman. Killing, that's all you seem to know."

"Sorry, I'll start your riding lessons tomorrow," Trent said as he mounted Tex.

"The Comanche attack is bad timing for you, brother," Pat said. "Just when you thought you were making progress."

Trent shook his head. "As I said before, it's a long way to California. Now let's go and see if there are some survivors."

"You know full well we won't find anyone alive at the wagons. If anyone lived through the attack, the Comanches would have taken them captive. If that's the case, they'll wish they were dead," Pat said before he spurred Leo lightly in the sides. The spotted mustang bolted forward as though from starting blocks.

"Showoff," Trent mumbled as he gave Tex free rein. The Appaloosa sprinted after Pat's mustang, with Lobo matching his pace.

When they topped a rise in the trail, the sight of twenty burning wagons greeted them. The wagons had burned for hours. Only the collapsed wooden frames of the wagons still smoldered. As the brothers approached, they came across the bodies of several men lying among the discarded supplies the Comanches didn't want.

Pat jumped off his horse and ran from body to body. "I don't see Digger Johnson," he called out when he finished examining the dead. "They took him and maybe five other men. What do you want to do?"

Trent took a deep breath. "We have to go after them. The Comanches will take their time killing them. We might be able to save a few." Trent shook his head. "I don't mind dying, Pat. But dang it, I don't want to die trying to save Digger Johnson. We can't just do nothing... Come on, let's track them down."

"It ain't going to be hard. I counted over forty horses in the war party. We're going to be in for a drag down fight when we catch them."

"I've got two extra boxes of shells, so the numbers are no problem," Trent said.

"High on yourself as always, brother," Pat said as they trotted in the direction the tracks led. Lobo followed close behind Tex. "I hope you have a plan besides using your rifle. We can't kill them all if they rush us, which they will the moment you open fire," Pad shouted as they followed the tracks over the open prairie.

"I'll take out their war chiefs while you move in closer," Trent said.

"You want me to walk into a hornet's nest?"

"I want you to rescue the survivors while I draw the Comanches to me. I'll kill enough Comanches so you'll have horses for the men who are still alive... if there are any."

"That's fine and dandy, but if Tex can't outrun their ponies, you're a dead man," Pat said.

"Tex isn't a sprinter like Leo, but he can run all day," Trent said.

"For this plan of yours to work, you need a high elevation to get some distance to shoot from, or else they'll be on you faster than a dog on a biscuit."

"That's going to be the problem," Trent acknowledged.

"You'll just have to shimmy up a tall pine tree if one is near their camp."

"They'll most likely camp near a stream. If so, we'll find trees," Trent shook his head. "That polecat Digger isn't worth all this trouble."

"Yup, but here we are," Pat said. "Fixing to get ourselves killed. I guess someone else will be teaching that gal of yours how to ride that Morgan."

"Pat, to hell with the Comanches. Maybe I'll just shoot your ornery hide," Trent said as he noticed a stand of pines in the distance. "I think we're approaching a stream."

Pat nodded. "Yup, the tracks are fresh, probably less than an hour old." He pointed to a pine that towered twenty-five feet above its companions. "That's your elevation."

"Hmm, I think my plan is a cockamamie one!" Trent said as he looked at the tall pine.

"Yup, I agree. I just can't come up with a better one."

"Dang it! Climbing is going to get pine resin all over Bruce's shirt!" Trent complained.

"Don't worry. Becky will boil it out in a washtub," Pat said as they dismounted.

Trent nodded. "Yeah, with me inside of it!"

Pat tossed Trent a length of rope. "Use this to sling your rifle over your shoulder."

"Speaking of shoulders, mine is still hurt where I got shot."

"You want to save Digger and his men or not?" Pat asked.

Trent took a deep breath. "Of course."

Pat pointed at the ponderosa. "Start climbing."

Trent didn't have to shimmy up far before he grabbed a limb. From then on, climbing was easy. When he climbed past the canopy of the other pines, he scanned the bank of the stream. Downstream, he spotted horses. A little further along, he saw about twenty Comanches sitting in a circle. In the middle, five men—one burly and bald—were tied to poles sticking out of the ground.

From a distance, Trent couldn't hear the yelling, but one of the Comanches held a man's entrails in his left hand. Having seen enough, Trent climbed two-thirds of the way back down the pine. "They're torturing one of Digger's men."

Lobo glanced up and whined at the sound of Trent's voice.

"He's a goner already, but if we move fast, we might save the other four. I think one of them is Digger. I spotted the war chief. I'll give you time to get in place before I put him and three more of the Comanches in the dirt. Then I'm going to climb down as fast as I can and hightail it upriver a ways before turning back to the wagons." Trent paused. "Get the men to the wagons and get ready for an assault."

Pat just nodded before he rode into the brush.

Trent figured he might not survive the action. But the thought of death didn't bother him. He put it out of his mind as he climbed up the pine. He could see Pat making his way along the riverbank of the meandering stream. Trent positioned himself on a branch and followed Pat through his rifle sight, in case he got in trouble with a sentry. He lost sight of Pat when he entered thick brush near the Comanches.

Trent turned his rifle sights onto the Comanches. The warrior with the knife was still working on the man he had disemboweled. Unfortunately, the poor soul being tortured was still alive. Trent could see the man's head jerking from side to side. Trent steeled himself and watched the man use his knife to inflict cuts on the man's body. However, the moment he figured Pat was in position, he squeezed the trigger, killing the war chief who stood supervising the man's torture.

Trent smiled when the war chief suddenly stood up on his tiptoes and grabbed his chest. The Comanches watched in silence as their chief fell backward onto the ground. Before the men sprang into action, Trent shot the torturer in the head. After that, it was like jabbing a stick in an anthill. Men ran in all directions as they tried to spot who had fired on them.

Trent put two more in the dirt before one of the Comanches pointed in Trent's direction. The moment that happened, Trent put his rifle over his shoulder and climbed down the tree like a squirrel with a weasel hot on its tail. The moment his feet hit the ground, Trent sprinted to Tex and vaulted into the saddle. Less than two minutes after firing his last shot, Trent reined his horse into the water and, with Lobo on his heels, headed upstream, hoping to slow down the pursuit. He left the stream after half a mile, and like a dog with his tail on fire, he lit out across the prairie.

Even though he couldn't hear the whooping men, he was certain they would be hightailing it after him soon. Taking to the stream had only bought him a little time. He didn't doubt they would quickly find Tex's tracks where he had left the stream. What Trent didn't hear were pistol shots. He smiled. Pat had gone full stealth and used his knife to dispatch any Comanches left to guard the prisoners. His brother was as deadly with a knife as he was with one of his Colts. He could kill a man with a knife throw twenty yards away.

Trent didn't push Tex to run all out. He let the Appaloosa choose his own pace. He glanced down at Lobo. The big dog ran smoothly beside the stallion. The wagons were at least ten miles across the prairie from the stream. Tex could maintain a quick trot for that distance but not a gallop. When he left the trees near the stream, Trent rode across the shadow of the rolling hills. He turned back in his saddle as he reached the top of one.

In the distance, he spotted the Comanches racing all out to catch him. He smiled. They were letting their emotions guide them instead of experience. Killing the war chief had served its purpose, as they were running their horses flat out. Sure, the Comanches were gaining on him now, but their horses would fade before they caught him. In three more miles, they would have to walk their winded mounts while Tex would still be trotting across the grassland.

So determined were some Comanches that they rode their ponies until they dropped while they attempted to close the distance. The better horses managed to close the gap. Still, Trent didn't urge Tex to a gallop. Instead, he turned in the saddle as the Comanches rode into the range of his .50 caliber Sharps but still out of Winchester range. He took careful aim.

He fired. The leading man slumped forward and slid off his horse. The Comanches shouted their defiance. Some whipped their horses, trying to get more speed out of the winded animals. Trent calmly reloaded. He chose one of the slower riders as his target and fired. The big caliber bullet knocked the Comanche backward off his horse. This time, he got the entire war party's attention as they realized they were all in range of the buffalo rifle. With his third shot, Trent killed the frontrunner.

The Comanches pulled up and sat astride their horses as they watched Trent urge Tex to a fast gallop which none of their exhausted horses could match. Trent smiled. He had broken the Comanches' will. They would abandon their pursuit.

"You can run all day too, Lobo," Trent told the wolf-dog.

Trent was mildly surprised to still be alive. He knew it was only because of Tex. The Appaloosa's stamina had saved his life. Realizing the danger from the Comanches had passed for the moment, Trent reined Tex in and walked him. His thoughts turned to Pat. He hoped his brother had been able to save the remaining captives. He wouldn't know the outcome until Pat returned to the wagon train.

Digger's wagons were still smoldering when Trent approached the sight of the Comanche ambush. As he rode, he spotted shovels and other tools the Comanches had deemed useless. Tomorrow, when the oxen wagon train got underway, they could pick through the tools and collect what was worthwhile.

Bruce and Jake hurried from the circled wagons to meet Trent as he dismounted.

"You're alive?" Bruce said. "I honestly didn't think I would see you again. But where's Pat?"

Trent shrugged. "I'm not sure. I lured the Comanches into chasing me. He was supposed to slip into their camp to release the surviving captives. We'll have to wait and see."

"I hope he survived," Jake said. "Unlike you, he seems like a fair fighting man."

Bruce glanced from Jake to Trent with a puzzled look on his face.

Trent chuckled. "I kicked him in the nuts during a fight in Independence. I didn't have time to give him a proper whupping."

"They are still sore!" Jake protested and let out a hardy laugh.

"Hmm, I'm glad that's water under the bridge. Come on, Trent. Lois cooked some biscuits and stew. I'm sure you're hungry."

"Yeah, I could eat an ox!" Trent said as he followed the two men inside the circle of wagons. "Let me unsaddle Tex, and I'll be over in a shake."

"Ah, that's what the women are cooking. The ox we lost in the storm," Jake said.

At the Cowans' wagon, Trent found Wes and Becky brushing their new horses. Wes hugged the red roan until he spotted Trent. "You made it back! I feared a Comanche would scalp you."

Trent removed his battered Boss of the Plains hat and ran his fingers through his blond hair. “Don’t you worry, pardner. I ain’t giving up my hair to no Comanche.”

“Hmm,” Becky said. “You need to give some of it up. Your hair is too long,”

“The next town we stop in, I’ll be sure to seek out a barber,” Trent said.

“Mama can cut your hair,” Wes said. “She cut mine. She placed a bowl over my head and cut around it. It’s nice, isn’t it?” Wes added.

Trent didn’t respond.

“Riders coming!”

Trent ran to the wagon in the direction of the Comanches, expecting to see the war party. “It’s Pat! And he’s got four men with him,” Trent shouted as he lowered his Sharps.

“He did it!” Bruce yelled as he joined Trent. “He saved some captives!”

“Seems that way,” Trent answered. “Hmm, it looks like Digger is one of the riders.”

“That man has the luck of the Irish,” Bruce shouted happily. “I thought for sure he was a goner.”

“A bad penny keeps showing up,” Trent said under his breath as Pat and the riders approached the wagons.

“God, ain’t you folks a sight for sore eyes,” Digger said as he climbed off the pony. “And I hope I never have to ride another horse bareback,” he added.

Trent noted that Doug, Digger’s driver, was among the other men. As he watched Doug dismount, the man dropped to his knees and kissed the ground. "If I ever make it back to Independence, I'll never come west again."

"Don't be so dramatic, Doug. You could get run over by a wagon in Independence," Digger said.

"Yes, but I won't get tortured like Gary. I'll take that image to my grave. Yessir. To my grave."

Trent glanced over at Digger. "Your wagons are all lost, along with most of your supplies."

"Yeah, I watched the heathens burn the wagons. When I get to Council Grove, I'm going to demand the army send soldiers out to punish them! They massacred fifteen of my men. They have to be made to pay!"

Pat shook his head. "They'll be halfway to Texas by the time the army sends troops. And if they do catch up with them, the Comanches will pick the soldiers off one at a time until they wipe them out."

"You're just saying that because you're half Indian, and you don't want to see your people killed," Digger snapped.

"Mister Johnson! You forget who saved your life!" Bruce said sternly. "If you plan on riding in my wagon train, show some respect or strike out on your own!"

"Your wagon train?" Digger said as his face turned scarlet.

"Yes, my wagon train. All your wagons are gone. And the good folks traveling with me elected me the wagon master today."

Chapter Eleven
Pistol Lessons

Wes jerked the old Colt Dragoon from his holster and shouted, "Bang! You're dead, Pat! I beat you to the draw!"

Pat twirled his Colts back into his holster.

"He's right!" Trent said. "The kid beat you to the draw."

Finally, Pat nodded. He was dressed in dungarees and Bruce's red shirt with a white headband. "Yup, I got beat on the draw by a kid. Shameful," he said, stone-faced. "It means I'm a good teacher. Of course, the kid can't shoot straight. In fact, he ain't fired the pistol."

"But I've been practicing firing," Wes said.

Trent shook his head. "Kid, you can't practice without shells."

"Yeah, I can. I aim and pull the trigger."

Pat shook his head, causing his long black hair to slap against the cheeks of his face. Trent took a deep breath.

"What's going on? Wes! What are you doing wearing a gun?" Bruce demanded as he walked up behind the three.

Wes glanced at the ground.

"He's learning to protect himself, Bruce. This isn't Boston. Here, a man must know how to handle a gun. His life depends on it," Trent said.

Bruce shook his head. "Dang it! He's just a boy!"

"No," Pat said. "Out West, Wes is considered a man. I'm only eighteen—three years older than Wes, myself."

Trent nodded. "Yeah, out here on the frontier, you have to grow up fast."

"You two went behind my back!" Bruce accused.

"Yup, we did," Trent said. "And when you're wrong, we'll do it again. You still think like a Bostonian. If you don't watch it, such thinking will get you and your family killed."

Bruce stood silent as he looked at Wes. "Is he any good with that pistol?"

Trent smiled. "He's faster on the draw than Pat. I never thought I would see someone quicker than my little brother."

Bruce glanced at Pat.

"Don't rub it in," Pat said without changing his facial expression.

"Let me see you draw," Bruce said and nodded at Wes.

The big Colt appeared in the boy's hand in a flash.

A shocked look distorted Bruce's friendly face. "I guess I've lost you, son. You're never going to till the soil with me on a homestead when you can pull a pistol that fast," Bruce said in a disappointed tone.

"Pa, I never did like working the garden at home," Wes said.

Bruce nodded. "Yeah, but I was hoping you would feel different when we staked out a claim." He took a deep breath before he turned to face Trent. "There' are a couple of wagons and some riders headed back to Independence from Council Grove. Digger Johnson and his men are going to join them. I thought you might want to know," he added as he turned to leave.

"Pa, wait up. I'll walk with you," Wes said as he hurried to his father's side. "Pa, are you mad at me?"

Bruce finally smiled. "No, it's just hard to see you grow up so fast. I guess I've been sheltering you too much."

"Should I take off my gun belt?"

"Is the pistol loaded?"

Wes shook his head. "Trent and Pat won't let me use shells."

"Then keep it on, but be prepared for your mother's scorn when she sees it," Bruce said as he headed toward the wagons.

"Pat, I guess we better go talk with the travelers. See what awaits us up the trail," Trent said as he fell in behind Bruce and Wes.

When they reached the wagons, Bruce and Wes headed for theirs. It was late, and Bruce had already circled the wagons. Those from Council Grove were outside the circle. The two prairie schooners' canvas tops had patches that covered rips. Teams of mules pulled both wagons. Trent counted six horses hobbled near the wagons to graze as he and Pat approached the strangers' campfire.

A tall, lanky, clean-shaven man stopped jawing with Digger Johnson. Four more strangers sat on the ground near the fire along with Digger's remaining men. The tall man gave Trent and Pat an unwelcome look. Trent noted he wore his gun belt low and his holster tied to his leg. The man didn't smile or offer a greeting.

"Howdy, pardner," Trent called out.

The man looked at Pat. "I don't like Indians."

Trent shrugged. "They probably don't like you either. My name is Trent, and this is my brother, Pat."

"They're both half-breeds," Digger said as he gave Trent a hard look.

The tall man said, "My name is Jack Blake. Maybe you've heard of me," he added.

Trent shook his head. "Nope." He glanced over at Pat. "How about you?"

"I might have seen his mug on a wanted poster," Pat said in his strange Texan drawl.

Jack stiffened. "I ain't on no wanted poster. But there's a bounty on the two of you half-breeds. A hundred dollars for each."

Trent glanced at Digger Johnson. "This is your doing!"

"I don't like to be threatened, especially by two no-account Yaqui," Digger spat out like venom.

Jack lowered his hand toward his Colt Army.

Pat drew his right pistol and fired.

"What the heck?" Jack shouted. He glanced down at his Colt. Pat's bullet had shattered the handle. His face paled when he saw Pat's pistol pointed at him.

Pat nodded at Trent. "Should I kill him and Digger?"

"I don't know. He says there ain't a reward on his ugly face," Trent replied. "And since you consider digging graves women's work, I would have to bury him. Why don't we just take their guns and keep them until they depart for Independence tomorrow? Trent nodded at Jack. "Just gather up his men's guns."

"You can't take our guns! There's a large gang of Texas outlaws on our trail. I killed two of the gang in the saloon in Council Grove. I fear they're tracking me," Jack pleaded.

Trent shifted his Sharps in the crook of his arm. "Pat, I do think they were going to keep that information under their hats."

"We should kill them all," Pat said.

Trent shook his head and motioned toward Jack. "Just gather their weapons. I want to get back to the Cowans' wagon. My belly is growling for some of Miss Lois's biscuits and bacon."

Digger pointed his finger at Trent. "I'll see that you never get to California. I'm going to put a thousand-dollar bounty on Pat, dead or alive! You two are the cause of me losing my wagons! You made me slow down for oxen-drawn wagons. I would have been in Council Grove by now, and the oxen wagons would be the ones the Comanches burned."

"Pat hasn't broken any laws," Trent said.

"He didn't have to. He looks like a Yaqui. The Mexican government has a bounty on Yaqui. I'll just add a little more money for Pat," Digger Johnson said with a sneer. "I'll issue it as a reward from the Mexican government and put my name on the wanted poster as the agent in charge of paying the bounty. I figure you'll protect your brother, Trent, and catch a bullet too."

Trent nodded. "Yup, I always knew you were a crook, Digger."

Pat, who had found a burlap bag inside the wagon, walked around collecting the men's guns.

"Well, now, Digger, you just cut your chances on making it back to Independence. I'm keeping your guns and ammo. You won't be getting them back come morning. Pat, go and search the wagon for shells and any hidden weapons," Trent said.

Jack Blake shook his head vigorously. "You can't do this! There are bandits galore between here and Kansas City! We'll be helpless if attacked."

Trent smiled. "Yup, you sure will. And if I were a gambling man, I'd wager you don't make it."

Digger Johnson shook his head. "I'll see you and your Yaqui brother put in the dirt."

"I found two boxes of rifle shells, three boxes of pistol shells, three Winchesters, and a Sharps buffalo rifle hidden under a blanket," Pat said as he climbed out of the wagon, loaded down with another burlap sack. He picked up the sack with the pistols and walked over to where Trent stood with his Sharps in the crook of his arm.

Trent nodded. "Good, now we can make sure everyone in the wagon train is armed to the teeth."

"And Wes will have plenty of ammo to practice shooting," Pat said as he walked past Trent, lugging the two sacks over his shoulder. "Come on. I'm hungry too."

"Mr. Trent!" Doug called out. "I want to join your train. I don't want to return to Independence." Digger's clerk walked away from the campfire. "I know how to use a Winchester. And I know how to work oxen."

"Doug! You get back here this minute! You work for me!" Digger yelled.

"No, Mister Johnson. Not anymore. Trent and Pat aren't the cause of you losing your wagons and almost getting us killed. It's all your fault. And I wash my hands of you," Doug said. He caught up with Trent and Pat. "Please, can I join you?"

Trent and Pat exchanged glances. "Sure!" Trent said. "Help Pat carry the burlap sacks."

"No," Pat said. "Go get one of their horses. You'll need it. Call it back-pay from Digger."

Trent nodded. "Good idea." He raised his voice. "Digger, Doug is taking one of your new friends' horses. Consider it back-pay. Oh yeah, I'll put a fist-size hole in anyone who tries to stop Doug," Trent added, shifting his Sharps in the crook of his arm.

"They hang horse thieves," Jack called out.

"Pat and I'll bare witness that instead of cash payment, Doug accepted a horse for his back wages," Trent said.

Both Jack and Digger looked surprised at Trent's statement.

"Hmm. Before he died, my father had hopes I would be a lawyer. He had me read every law book he could get his hands on. But I loved my Sharps too much to trade it in for a desk job," Trent said as Doug walked up, leading a steel-dust gelding. "I would wish you all good luck on the trek back to Independence, but to be honest, I hope you don't make it."

Chapter Twelve
Texas Bandits

"I still can't believe you and Pat took those men's guns and sent them down the trail unarmed," Bruce said as Trent walked alongside him while he drove the oxen.

"Digger paid that gunslinger to kill Pat and me. And he said he was going to issue a wanted dead or alive poster on Pat when he returned to Independence. I should have put him in the dirt," Trent said.

Bruce shook his head. "I doubt he makes it."

"I don't know, Bruce. We've pretty much cleared out the bandits from here to Independence."

"I heard pistol fire early this morning," Bruce said. "Is Pat teaching Wes to shoot?"

"The kid is amazing. He has a good eye to go along with his quick hands. He didn't need much teaching. He can hit center already," Trent said. "Pat gave him Jack Blake's Peacemaker. He handles it like he was born with it in his hand."

Bruce shook his head. "I've lost my boy. When you put a pistol in his hand, he became a man."

"Bruce, it was always going to happen. He never was going to be a farmer," Trent said.

"His mother cried," Bruce admitted. "And I felt like it."

"Sorry," Trent said.

"Where's Pat?"

"He rode ahead with Doug to scout."

Bruce cracked his whip over the backs of the oxen. "Do you trust Doug? He's one of Digger's men."

"Not completely. But I'm not worried. Pat will keep an eye on him."

"Are you concerned about this Texas gang?"

"Yup, that's why I sent Pat out to scout. He'll ride a day or two ahead of us. If he spots signs of the outlaws, he'll send Doug back to warn us while he watches them," Trent said.

"You must be mighty worried about these Texans. That's why you distributed the Winchesters to the other men and me."

"It's better to be prepared for the worst," Trent said.

"Trent!" Becky called as she rode up on her morgan mare. "Let's ride ahead. I want to gallop, Lady."

Trent glanced down at Bruce.

Bruce nodded. "Yeah, go on. She's in safe hands. If you don't go with her, she's liable to light out on her own."

"Thanks, Pa," Becky said.

"Like I have a choice?" Bruce called after them as they rode ahead.

"Don't you get tired of carrying that heavy rifle all the time?" Becky asked as they trotted side by side.

"Nope, I feel naked without it. Anyway, I never know when I'll need it."

"When you settle down on a farm, you can plow the fields holding a rifle," Becky said and snickered.

“I don’t plan on farming. It’s too much work and too little money,” Trent said.

“So what do you plan to do with your life, Trent?” Becky demanded.

“Maybe I’ll pan for gold in California?” Trent said.

“Hmm, that’s the dumbest thing I’ve ever heard. Your chances of finding gold are about the same as drawing four aces in a card game,” Becky said. She urged her mare into a full gallop.

“Women,” Trent said under his breath as he gave Tex his head.

As Trent rode after Becky, he wondered why settlers didn’t just stay on the prairie between Kansas City and Council Grove. The land looked suitable for farming. He figured it was the Kiowas and Comanches that kept pilgrims from staking homesteads along this section of the Santa Fe Trail.

“Hey, we should turn back,” Trent called out an hour later as they walked their horses side by side. “It's going to take a while to get back. We must walk the horses. They’re winded.”

“I never felt so free as I do while riding Lady,” Becky said as she turned her mount around. “Thanks for giving me a horse, Trent.”

Trent smiled. “You needed one, as did Wes.”

“I never thought I would like riding a horse. I guess I was so used to being driven in a carriage in Boston that it never entered my mind to use a horse,” Becky said as they slowly made their way back to the wagons. “What do you think Pa’s chances are of finding a good piece of land in Texas?" she added.

"The part of Texas that the Santa Fe Trail cuts through is pretty dry country. It's more suited for cattle than farming. I figure Bruce is going to be disappointed. The eastern part is rolling hills, but the western part is flat and treeless. The two parts are divided by deep canyons. The ranchers in that part of Texas don't cotton to settlers."

"You seem to know a lot about Texas."

"Yup, Pat and I traveled most of Texas as my father traded with the small settlements all over. I was born in Texas, as was Pat."

Two hours later, they approached the wagons. Wes spotted them and came racing out to meet them on his quarter horse. "Pa's been worried."

"As long as I got my Sharps, there's no call for him to worry about Becky's safety," Trent said.

"Yeah, well, you need to tell him that. I did, and he still worried," Wes said.

Trent had to admit the kid had changed since he put on a gun belt. He seemed less carefree.

"He's going to bark at you some, Trent," Wes warned as Becky trotted ahead to tie her horse to the back of the wagon and join her mother inside.

"Right," Trent said as they approached Bruce.

"That was some ride. I thought you decided to go all the way to Council Grove," Bruce said as he snapped his whip.

"Becky was enjoying herself. I didn't want to tell her to turn back until I thought we must," Trent said.

"Yeah, well, don't ride so far the next time," Bruce said.

Trent tipped his hat. "Yes, sir."

"Isn't that Pat and Doug?" Wes said, pointing up the trail.

"Yup, and they're in a hurry."

"That ain't good," Bruce said. "Dang it. If we aren't in the fire, we're in the frying pan."

Trent shook his head. "We don't know that for a fact, Bruce."

"Oh, yes, we do, and you know it," Bruce answered.

Trent shrugged. "Let's just wait and see what Pat has to say before we jump the gun."

Wes touched the handle of his Peacemaker. "Don't worry, Pa. I'll protect the family."

Bruce smiled weakly. "Yeah, Wes, I guess you would give it a go. But shooting a man is different from shooting a tin can."

"Yeah, Pa. A man can move, and a tin can can't."

Trent chuckled.

Bruce shook his head. "It ain't funny."

The conversation died as Pat and Doug stopped their horses and dismounted.

"What did you find that lit your tail on fire?" Trent asked.

"Jack Blake spoke the truth. I spotted a large group of mounted men camped about a mile north of the trail. I followed one of their lookouts back to their hideout in a dry wash. They're watching the trail. They mean to attack any wagons that pass by."

"How many?" Bruce asked in a panicked voice.

"I counted forty," Pat replied. "Some of them wore sombreros. I'm guessing they're the outfit from Texas."

Bruce shook his head as he walked around in a circle. He finally stopped. "We can't fight off forty men!" He glanced over at Trent. "I don't want to turn back. And we can't stay here. They're liable to send out scouts and find us."

Trent nodded. "Go and have everyone circle the wagons. I'll jaw with Pat and see if we can come up with a plan."

"I don't know of a plan that can neutralize forty armed men," Bruce said.

"That's because you aren't half Yaqui," Pat said. He nodded at Doug. "Go and help them with the oxen."

Wes stayed behind.

Pat glanced at the boy with a questioning look.

"I'm in on whatever you all plan. I'm not staying back with the wagons," Wes said in a determined voice.

"You see what you created, Pat?" Trent said.

Pat nodded. "Yeah, if he weren't so good with that Colt, I would spank his britches." He took a deep breath. "Actually, we might need an extra man."

"What about Doug?" Trent asked.

Pat shook his head. "I don't trust him. I felt like a cat around a dog the entire time. I didn't dare take my eyes off him for fear he would shoot me in the back."

"Hmm, he had me fooled," Trent said.

"We should shoot him," Wes said.

"Kid," Trent said. "We should call you weasel, you're so bloodthirsty."

Wes shook his head. "I dang sure don't like that. I'm gonna make a name for myself as the Boston Kid."

"Well, now that's a name if I ever heard one," Trent said. "Just saying it scares the crawdads out of me," he added and chuckled.

"You want to hear my plan, Trent, or tease the kid?" Pat said.

"Well, I guess I better listen to your plan before you get your blood riled up," Trent said. "Shoot!"

"We steal their horses!" Pat said.

Trent arched his eyebrows. "Steal their horses. You sure you didn't get too much sun, Pat?"

"It's a good plan," Pat said. "The outlaws are camped in a dry wash about a mile from the trail. I guess they don't want their campfire spotted at night by an approaching wagon train. They keep their horses tied on a picket line at night. I saw it. All we have to do is sneak in, cut the line, and spook the horses. Then they'll be on foot."

Trent shook his head. "I've got a better idea. Since the horses are tied to a picket line, we cut the line and take their horses. Forty horses would fetch a good price in Council Grove."

"Forty horses are too many to rope together. It won't work."

"Divide them into three groups. That's about thirteen horses each. We all lead a group of horses out from the camp," Wes said.

"From the mouth of a babe," Trent said.

"Hmm," Pat said as he nodded his head. "It might work. But doing that will take more time than just cutting the rope and spooking the horses. It's riskier."

"But we can do it, right?" Trent said.

"Yeah, I guess we could. I can take care of the sentries. But I still think trying to lead the horses away is not going to work. The horses will resist. It'll slow us down. The outlaws could swarm over us before we get out of their hideout," Pat said.

Trent shrugged. "Then what?"

"We drive the horses down the wash. It goes for a couple of miles. When we come onto the prairie, we herd them back to the wagons. We'll lose some of them, but that doesn't matter. The outlaws will be afoot."

"Even without horses, they can still attack the wagons," Wes said.

Trent nodded. "Yeah, but it's better facing forty men on foot than mounted. I can kill quite a few before they get in Winchester range. Maybe pick off the head honcho and they'll think twice about fighting."

"The leader is a tall Texan with a tan slouch hat. He wears two guns like me," Pat said.

"Okay, I'll shoot anyone who wears a double holster," Trent said.

"It's a solid plan," Wes said, sounding much older than his years. "Pa will like it."

Trent shook his head. "No, Wes, we aren't gonna tell anyone. About midnight, the three of us are going to saddle our horses and sneak out of camp."

Wes nodded. "Sure, Trent, if that's what you want to do."

"It is. Not a word to anyone. Sleep in your normal place. Pat will come by to wake you when it's time to leave," Trent added.

"I'm a light sleeper," Wes said.

"Okay, go on and help your pa with the oxen," Trent said.

Pat stood rubbing his mustang on the shoulder until Wes walked out of hearing. "You ain't taking him with us, are you Trent?"

"Nope!"

Chapter Thirteen
Midnight Raid

The head of a Mexican man wearing a poncho drooped forward as he dozed. He sat on a boulder. Before him stood forty horses tied to a picket line. The moonlight revealed various colors and sizes. Most stood with one of their back legs bent. Others rested straight legged. All in all, it was a fine remuda.

The sentry stirred in his sleep. He lifted his head as though a noise had disturbed him. He must have sensed danger. He reached for his pistol. However, after the sharp blade of Pat's knife passed across his throat, the fingers that grasped for the pistol's handle went dead. Pat pulled the dead man's body off the boulder and laid him on the grass.

One of the horses, a buckskin, stomped his foot. Otherwise, the horses didn't react to the killing. Pat stood motionless while he listened. Except for crickets and an occasional howl of a coyote, the night was silent. After he convinced himself the killing of the guard had gone unnoticed, Pat cupped his hands over his mouth and gave the cry of a whippoorwill.

A moment later, Trent walked up, leading Tex and Leo.

"All's clear," Pat whispered. "Let's cut them loose and head for the hills!"

"Is he the only sentry?"

Pat nodded, then realized Trent probably couldn't see the movement. "Yes."

"Let's cut them free," Trent said.

Suddenly, the cocking of a dozen Winchester rifles caused the two brothers to freeze.

"Well, well, what do we have here? Horse thieves?" a voice with a deep Texan drawl said. "I must admit, that was pretty fine work the way the Yaqui dispatched Valdez. Of course, he wasn't worth his salt."

"Juan, get their weapons," a tall Texan wearing a slouch hat ordered. "Be careful with the Yaqui. He's a killer if I ever laid eyes on one."

"Why not just shoot them?" a short man with a handlebar mustache said.

"No, we'll hang them at daybreak. And then attack their wagon train," the tall Texan said as a man bought up a lantern. "I see blondie is surprised I know about the wagon train." The man pulled out a spyglass and extended it to full length. "I've been watching you all from afar."

Trent and Pat exchanged glances.

"When I saw you circle the wagons, I figured you had located my camp and might try something tonight. I expected all your men to attack. But you surprised me by going after the horses. Which was a great plan if it had worked."

"What's your name?" Trent asked.

"Curt Cutler. With all the wanted posters floating around with my picture on them, I'm surprised you have to ask."

"I've heard the name. You've been hitting Mexican-owned ranches in Texas," Trent said.

"I raided only the Mexican ranches until Texas sent lawmen to arrest me. Now, I take what I want from both Mexicans and Texans," Curt said.

"What? Did it get too hot for you down Texas way?" Trent said as Juan took his Sharps.

Juan motioned to another outlaw. "Shorty, take the Yaqui's weapons."

"Tie them to the big ponderosa, and let's all get a little shut-eye before its daylight," Curt ordered. "We'll hang them after breakfast."

"We should just cut their throats like they did Valdez," Juan said as he tied Trent's hands behind his back. "They're dangerous. I've heard of the Yaqui brothers. They leave a trail of bodies wherever they go."

"Just do as you are told, Juan. I ain't seen a hanging in a coon's age. I want to see them swing from the ponderosa," Curt ordered. "And you can keep watch over them."

"Make a sudden move, Yaqui, and I'll cut your throat anyway," Juan said as he pushed Trent toward a huge pine tree at the side of the dry wash. "I'm going to tie you standing up. Put a rope around your neck and legs. Your last night ain't going to be comfortable."

Neither Trent nor Pat spoke as Shorty and Juan tied them on the opposite sides of the tree. Shorty left, but Juan leaned his back against a rock and pulled his hat down over his face.

"This ain't good," Trent whispered.

"We're still alive," Pat replied.

Juan lifted his hat. "One more word out of you two, and I gag you both!"

Trent sighed. He could feel Pat testing the ropes. Trent didn't bother. He had seen how well Shorty tied Pat and knew it was useless to try to slip out of the ropes. Trent closed his eyes and tried to relax.

***

Something tapped the toe of Trent's boot. He glanced down. The moonlight played across Wes's upraised face. The boy put his finger to his lips. He showed Pat's knife, which he held in his hand, and nodded toward Juan.

Trent tried to shake off Wes. The boy was going to get himself killed trying to save him and Pat. The boy had never knifed a man...

In dismay, he watched as Wes crept over behind Juan. Then Wes paused as though he didn't know what to do next. He glanced at Trent. In the moonlight, Trent saw Wes shrug as he reached over and brought the knife down near the outlaw's neck.

He's going to get himself killed for sure!

Wes suddenly wrapped his left hand around Juan's hat-covered face as he slid the blade of Pat's knife across the man's throat. He held on as Juan made a moaning sound into his hat while kicking out with his legs. It was over in a few seconds.

Wes let go of Juan and staggered back. The kid looked like he was fixing to vomit. Then he shook his head and stumbled over to the pine. Trent could feel the boy's hands tremble as he cut the ropes.

Once he freed Trent and Pat, Wes seemed recovered. He pointed over to where he had deposited Trent's Sharps and Pat's pistols. Trent hurried over and grabbed his Sharps while Pat strapped on his guns.

"Horses," Pat whispered and headed back to where the horses were tied to the picket line. Pat suddenly held up his hand. He leaned his head near Wes. "Give me my knife."

Wes relinquished the knife.

Pat took it and disappeared among the rocks. A few moments later, he suddenly appeared in front of them. "Now, let's cut the horses loose and head for the wagons."

"Good they didn't unsaddle our horses," Trent whispered as he untied Tex from the picket line. He watched Pat move from horse to horse, cutting the ropes that bound them.

Wes sat on Major as though in a daze.

A few minutes later, Trent saw Pat's arm pump in the dim moonlight. He raised his Sharps and fired into the air as Pat fired his pistols. The remuda of horses stampeded down the wash in the opposite direction of the outlaws' camp. Trent and Pat yelled as they raced behind the horses.

Wes rode silently as Major followed the stampeding horses on his own accord.

Pistol shots rang out as the outlaws spilled out of camp like swarming ants. Trent heard men yelling as they attempted to pursue the horses. However, the noise of the outlaws vanished as the herd of horses galloped down the dry wash. Trent let them run until they were winded. Only after the horses emerged from the wash did Trent, Pat, and Wes herd them toward the wagons.

Daylight found the three men within sight of the wagons. Everyone stood watching as Trent left the herd with Pat and Wes, who had recovered from the shock of killing Juan.

"What in blazes have you gone and done?" Bruce demanded as Trent stopped his horse in front of the Cowans' wagon.

"We stole the outlaw's horses."

"You took Wes with you? You could have gotten him killed," Bruce snarled.

Trent shook his head. "Nope, we left him here. He followed us later, and it's a good thing he did. He saved Pat and me from a hangman's noose."

"What are you talking about?" Bruce demanded.

"The outlaws captured us. Wes sneaked into their camp. He found our weapons and then killed the sentry posted to watch us."

"Wes?" Bruce said.

"Yup, your son. He did a foolish but brave thing. Could have gotten himself shot," Trent admitted.

Bruck shook his head. "He killed a man?"

Trent glanced to the ground. "He had to."

Bruce took a deep breath. "He'll never be the same."

Trent nodded. "I reckon you're right. He seemed to take killing the guard hard for a time. But he seems himself again."

"The outlaws will come for their horses," Ralf said as he joined them.

"Which would you rather face, men on horseback or afoot?" Trent asked the big man. "And we'll herd the horses inside the wagon's circle. If they attack, they're likely to shoot their own horses. That's going to prey on their minds. It will make them hesitate."

"They'll attack anyway," Bruce declared.

Trent nodded. "But if they lose enough men, they might parley with us."

Bruce shook his head. "We could never trust them."

Trent nodded. "However, if we return their horses in exchange for their guns, we don't need to trust them."

"You think they'll give up their weapons?" Bruce asked.

"Cowboys don't like to walk, and outlaws like it even less," Trent said. "Of course, we have to weather their first assault."

"How many outlaws?" Ralf asked.

"Almost forty," Trent replied.

"That's four-to-one," Bruce said.

"We have the protection of the wagons and the horses. They're gonna be out in the open," Trent said.

"They'll wait and attack at night," Ralf said. "That's what I would do."

"We can't let them do that," Trent said. "They'd swarm us in the dark. If we have the lanterns lit, it'll be a bullseye for them to aim at."

Bruce shook his head. "We're done for."

"I've got another idea. It's a harsh one. But it's the only way to stop them," Trent said.

Bruce sighed. "Okay, let's hear it."

"We treat them like they were a herd of buffalo," Trent said.

"What are you talking about?" Ralf asked with a puzzled look on his face.

"Pat and I use the Sharps and shoot them from a distance. Pick them off one at a time and keep moving out of Winchester range," Trent said. "Pat from the rear and me from the front. We wait until they move out of the wash and onto the prairie. They won't have any cover. It'll be like shooting buffalo."

"But that's cold-blooded murder," Bruce protested.

Trent nodded. "Yup, but the alternative is to let them overrun the wagons tonight. Do you realize what they would do to your wife and daughter, Bruce?"

"It's still murder," Bruce said.

"Stuff your Boston morality in a tobacco can," Ralf said. "I'm not letting them have their way with my wife!"

"Bruce, we don't have a choice," Trent said.

"I don't like it. But I don't want anything to happen to Lois or Becky," Bruce said.

"I'm taking that as approval," Trent said. "Ralf, do you have a horse? I need someone to help Wes with the horses."

"No, but Phillip Ganger has one. I'll borrow it."

Trent nodded. "Saddle it up. I'm going to fetch Pat. Get out to help Wes as soon as you can."

"Do you want me to keep the wagons circled?" Bruce asked.

"No, you head out as soon as you can. The wagon trail is the bait to draw them out of the wash in broad daylight. They aren't going to want to wait until the wagon train stops for the night. They'll have to walk too far. Curt Cutler will see the wagons moving through his spyglass and order his gang to move into position beside the trail. When they're all far enough out of the wash, they can't hurry back to safety, Pat and I will start shooting," Trent explained.

Bruce shook his head. "I still don't like the idea of killing men, even outlaws, from a distance."

"It's the only way," Trent said. "I better go and fetch the other Sharps and all the ammo."

Chapter Fourteen
Like Shooting Buffalo

Trent stood up in his stirrups and looked at the opening of the wash. "Here they come."

"I'm going to kill that guy Shorty, for sure," Pat said. "I still have a rope burn around my neck. I think if Wes hadn't rescued us, I would have choked to death."

"I'm going to try my best to put Curt Cutler in the dirt," Trent said. "You circle to the rear, and I'll wait here. We'll catch them in a crossfire. Shoot as fast as you can reload."

"What if some run for the safety of the dry wash and the other press the attack on the wagons?"

"We'll have them trapped between us. Either way they run, they'll be in our killing field."

"Bruce didn't like the plan," Pat said.

"Yeah, well, I don't particularly like it either. But the outlaws are bringing it on themselves," Trent said.

"I'll circle around. When I hear your shot, I'll start shooting from behind." Pat spurred Leo lightly. The big spotted mustang broke into a fast trot.

Trent followed Pat's progress until he dipped over the hill. He glanced in the direction of the mouth of the dry wash. *Curt probably had his spyglass out. He thinks Pat and I are scouts to warn the wagons when his men attack. It's going to shock him when we start firing the buffalo rifles.*

Twenty minutes later, Trent spotted a line of outlaws heading toward the wagons. The men walked with carefree strides toward the trail to an intercept course with the wagons. They approached Trent's position as though they expected him to break and ride back to the wagons.

Trent didn't move his Sharps from the crook of his arm until the outlaws approached within four hundred yards of where he sat astride Tex. The men had formed a line to intimidate the settlers in the wagons.

"Let's see who intimidates who," Trent said under his breath as he lifted the rifle to his shoulder.

He took careful aim. He didn't want to miss his first shot. Luckily, the men were walking straight toward him. He didn't have to lead them with his shot. Finally, Trent squeezed the trigger. He felt the familiar kick into his shoulder as the explosive sound of the Sharps echoed across the prairie. One of the outlaws in the center of the line of men stiffened and fell backward.

"Gotcha!" Trent said as he reloaded. He had just finished chambering another round when the loud crack of another Sharps reached his ears. Another man in the advancing line fell face down in the grass.

The picket line halted.

Trent aimed and fired. Another outlaw slumped over and stayed down. Trent could see the panic sweep through the men as he aimed and fired again. His bullet took down another of the outlaws. The rest kissed the dirt. But still, Pat's shot struck one of the outlaws.

Even though they were out of effective range of their Winchesters, those who had them started firing. The muzzle fire gave the outlaws' positions away. Trent fired, reloaded, and fired again, silencing a rifleman's fire with each shot.

Someone must have given an order to charge. Suddenly the outlaws sprung to their feet and rushed toward Trent's position. Trent calmly sat astride Tex and fired his Sharps as fast as he could reload. Pat kept up a steady line of fire from the rear. Men dropped like flies. Only when bullets kicked up dust within twenty yards of his position did Trent turn Tex around and ride to a safe distance. From his new position, he resumed his deadly rifle fire.

Finally, with half their number cut down by fire from the buffalo rifles, the men sought what little cover the grass gave them. Trent kept firing where he suspected outlaws had taken cover. Pat followed his example.

Finally, Curt Cutler raised his hand and waved a white handkerchief in the air. Trent stopped firing, as did Pat from the rear.

Cutler stood with his hands raised. Trent motioned the leader of the outlaws to walk toward him. He kept a bead on the man as he approached within forty yards of his position.

"That's far enough! Make a sudden move, and I'll put a blue whistler between your eyes."

"I've never seen someone shoot a rifle like you and your brother. I underestimated you two Yaquis," Curt yelled. "You've killed at least twenty of my men."

"That leaves twenty more to go," Trent called back. "And my brother and I have plenty of ammo and daylight left."

"Let's make a deal?" Curt yelled.

"The deal is this. You and your boys unbuckle your gun belts and toss them in a stack along with your rifles. Then you leave your weapons. Take your boots off and walk back to your camp," Trent shouted.

"And if I refuse?" Curt called back.

"Then my brother and I'll kill the other twenty members of your gang, including you," Trent said. "Your choice. Myself, I hope you don't take the deal. I'd rather kill lowdown coyotes like you and your men than let you live," Trent said.

"You're a curly wolf," Curt called back.

Trent glanced down at Lobo, who sat on his haunches. "He's got that right," Trent mumbled. "Deal or no deal?" Trent shouted.

"You aren't going to try to arrest us for the bounties?" Curt asked.

"Nope, but when I get to Council Grove, I'll spread the word where twenty unarmed outlaws with bounties on their heads are for the picking."

"I could offer you money..." Curt shouted.

"You could, but I wouldn't take it. Now, make up your mind. My brother's impatient. He's liable to start shooting again," Trent said.

"Deal, goldarn it!" Curt yelled angrily.

"Then unbuckle your gun belt, drop it and your spyglass. Walk back to your men and have them pile their gun belts, rifles, and boots on the ground. Then you and your men start walking back to your camp in the dry wash. If I spot anyone packing a pistol or rifle, he's a dead man!" Trent yelled.

Trent watched as the outlaws shucked their weapons and piled them in a stack. Then, one by one, they took off their boots. "Okay, start walking back to your camp," he called out once they finished.

Trent watched carefully as the men glanced at each other but held their position. Only when Curt started walking, did the men follow. Trent noticed one of the men walked stiff-legged, Trent shaded his eyes with his hand and squinted.

"Lobo, it looks like one of the outlaws has his rifle stuck down the leg of his dungarees," Trent said. He lifted his Sharps to his shoulder, took aim, and fired. At the loud crack of the buffalo rifle, the man with the limp fell face down into the grass. The entire gang stopped. "I said no weapons!" Trent yelled. "Shuck your weapons or die!" he added. At least four men pulled pistols out of the front of their shirts and tossed them on the ground.

"Pat will be watching you from the rim of the wash with the spyglass. Any man seen with a weapon will be shot," Trent shouted.

"I hope you rot in hell!" Curt Cutler yelled.

Once the Texan and his men disappeared into the dry wash, Trent turned his mount around and headed for the wagon train. Tex signaled he wanted to run, so Trent gave the Appaloosa his bit. It felt good to feel the wind against his face as the stallion raced across the prairie.

When he reached the first wagon, he found it belonged to Bruce. The Bostonian turned at the sound of Tex galloping. He waved to Trent with his free hand. The other one held his whip.

"I heard an awful lot of rifle shots," Bruce said. "Please tell me you didn't kill so many men."

"We did, and I don't regret it, Bruce. Curt Cutler and his gang have massacred countless ranchers down Texas way. The ones Pat and I shot deserved a visit with the hangman, but I guess a bullet will have to do," Trent said.

"Where's your brother?" Lois asked from the wagon seat.

"He'll hang around for a bit and watch them. I need several burlap bags. I've got to ride back and collect their boots and weapons. We're gonna have more guns than we know what to do with." Trent paused. "Where's Becky?"

"She rode out to help Wes and Doug herd the horses," Bruce said. "Dang it if she hasn't taken to the saddle awful quick," Bruce added and shook his head. "I guess I raised a gunslinger and a cowgirl." Bruce winked at Trent. "After this trek, Becky isn't gonna settle for some rich dandy."

Trent's face turned a shade redder.

"I'll fetch the burlap bag," Lois said and disappeared into the wagon.

Bruce said, "I can't believe we've run into so much trouble, and we ain't even made it to Council Grove. Heck, from what I've been told, the Santa Fe Trail gets worse past Council Grove. I reckon if I had known the adversity we would face, I would have just settled in Missouri."

"We've run into a streak of bad luck. But the Santa Fe Trail is dangerous. It's lined with the graves of settlers who didn't make it to California. But you're correct. The trail gets more dangerous the farther west you travel. The panhandle of Texas is a battleground between the whites and Apaches, who have the upper hand right now."

"It doesn't sound like Texas is suitable for homesteading," Bruce said.

"Staking a claim would be risky. It's ranch country. The ranchers don't cotton to sodbusters. So you'll have Apaches on the one hand and the ranchers cutting your fences on the other," Trent said. "But you'll fall in love with the high plains."

"Here are four burlap bags," Lois said as she emerged from the covered wagon.

Trent rode over and took the sacks. "Thanks, Miss Lois."

"Do you think we're free of the gang?" Lois asked.

"Yup, I believe so. They don't have guns, boots, or horses. There ain't much they can do but sit and wait for the sheriff in Council Grove to ride out and arrest them."

"Are there bounties on them?" Lois asked.

"We ain't taking any bounty money!" Bruce said in a loud and determined tone.

"Bruce is right. We aren't bounty hunters. What we did, we had to do to protect the wagon train," Trent said. "Well, if you'll excuse Lobo and me. We better get on back and collect the weapons and boots."

"I'm surprised the dog hasn't run off and joined a pack of wolves. I hear them howling at night," Lois said.

"He has a pack," Trent said. "We're his pack."

"Yup," Bruce said as he cracked his whip to keep the oxen moving. "And Trent is the leader of the pack."

Chapter Fifteen
A Rattlesnake

"What are we going to do with the horses?" Bruce asked while they sat around the campfire, eating biscuits and stew from the ox that died during the tornado.

Trent shoved a spoonful of stew in his mouth. "We divide them up between the wagons. Tie them behind the wagons during the day. At night, everyone will be responsible for hobbling their horses so they can graze during the night."

"I don't know how to hobble a horse, and I'm sure others don't either," Bruce said.

"Pat and I will show y'all how," Trent replied between spoons of stew.

"Do we take them all the way to California?" Wes asked.

"I don't advise it," Pat spoke up. "Best sell them in Council Grove."

"Why?" Bruce asked.

Pat nodded at Trent.

"The grass is good here," Trent picked up the conversation. "The horses can graze at night and have a belly full in no time. But Texas is dryer, and beyond even more so. There won't be enough grass to sustain the horses in the drier areas. And if we take the Cimarron Cutoff, we'll be traveling through the desert. Would have to haul oaks for them."

"I've heard the Cimarron Cutoff is more dangerous than sticking to the main trail," Bruce said.

"It is, but it cuts ten days off the journey. And the main trail heads into the mountains. Your oxen would have a difficult time there. You risk losing some, and if that happens, you have to abandon your wagon."

"I heard there are more Indians along the Cimarron Cutoff," Bruce stated and glanced over at Trent to see his reaction.

"Apaches. Yes, the trail goes through their land. They're on the warpath and very dangerous. However, there are grizzly bears in the mountains, timber wolves... cougars. Ah, plus more Indians. But we don't have to decide on which trail to take, yet. And I'm pretty sure we'll team up with a larger wagon train in Council Grove. It'll be up to the wagon master to decide which trail we take."

Lois shook her head. "I don't know about joining another wagon train. We barely survived joining Mister Johnson's."

"He wasn't a good man," Trent admitted. "And he didn't know much about the trail. The folks we meet in Council Grove will be more seasoned. They won't be from the east but mostly from Missouri and Kansas, wanting to push on to California."

"You mean they won't be tenderfoots like me," Bruce said.

Trent just smiled.

"I do want to get to California," Becky spoke up. "I've seen enough of the savage West. Men killing men. I want to live in a big city like Los Angeles or San Francisco, where men are gentlemen."

The smile dropped off Trent's face.

Wes shook his head. "I don't want to go to California. I want to stay in Texas or the Oklahoma territories. Or Arizona."

"Wes," Lois said. "I thought you'd had enough of the West too."

Wes shook his head. "I did feel bad about killing that sentry, Mama. But he deserved it. I know now that some men deserve to live, and some don't."

Bruce glanced at Trent. "How far are we from Council Grove?"

"Two days by wagon train."

"I look forward to a bath. I hope they have a bathhouse," Becky said.

"If we sell the horses, maybe we can afford to stay in a hotel for one night," Lois said.

"Yes, Mama, to sleep in a real bed!" Becky said hopefully.

Bruce nodded. "I reckon we could. We'll need to stock up on supplies."

"You'll also need to add a couple more water barrels to each of your wagons," Trent said.

"Trent, are you and Pat going to continue traveling with the wagon train?" Wes asked.

Trent and Pat exchanged glances. Trent nodded. "Yup, we'll make enough money selling our share of the horses to see us through for a while."

"Couldn't you collect some reward money on the outlaws?" Wes asked.

"We aren't bounty hunters," Pat said.

Wes shook his head. "Well, I would take it. I don't see anything wrong with collecting a bounty on the outlaw I killed!"

"It's getting late," Bruce said. "Let's all turn in for the night."

"Come along, Becky and Wes," Lois said as she stood up.

"I'm bunking under the wagon with Trent and Pat," Wes said.

"Come on, Becky," Lois said with a disappointed look.

Bruce glanced questioningly at Wes.

"Pa, I'm not a kid anymore," Wes stated.

Bruce gave Trent a hard look. "Yeah, right Wes. You've grown up fast."

"I'll take care of the fire," Trent said as Bruce stood.

"Then goodnight," Bruce said before he turned and walked to the wagon.

"Trent, I've been thinking. I want to be a bounty hunter," Wes said.

"You'll have to kill a lot of men, Wes," Pat said.

Wes shook his head. "If they're meant for the gallows, it doesn't matter none."

"Bounty hunters usually wind up with a bullet in the back," Trent said.

Wes shrugged. "I'll watch my back."

"Grab your saddle and bedroll," Trent said as he poured the remaining coffee on the fire.

Pat waited until Wes was out of earshot. "The Boston Kid, bounty hunter."

Trent shook his head. "It's our fault," he said as he stood. Lobo, who had been lying at Trent's feet, jumped up.

Pat shook his head. "Nope, the kid had it in him all the time. Maybe what we've taught him will keep him alive."

Wes was already asleep on his bedroll with his head on his saddle when Trent and Pat crawled under the wagon. Lobo moved over and waited for Trent to join him.

"I hope he learns how to sleep with one eye open," Trent whispered. He patted Lobo on the back as he laid his head on his saddle.

Wes opened one eye. "I heard that."

***

A loud piercing scream jarred Trent awake. He sat up, only to bang his head on the bottom of the wagon. "Ouch!"

A second scream echoed among the wagons.

"That's Becky!" Wes shouted as he crawled out from under the wagon and raced in the direction of the screams.

Trent and Pat sprinted after him.

"Becky!" Wes shouted as he spotted his sister limping toward the wagons.

"What happened?" Trent demanded as he reached Becky's side.

"A rattlesnake! It bit me. My ankle," Becky said as she pointed to her right leg.

"Sit down," Pat ordered as he pulled his knife.

"What... what are you going to do?" Wes asked when he spotted the knife.

"I'm going to cut the wound and suck out the poison."

"Cut me? No, no." Becky said as she collapsed onto the grass.

"Pat knows what he's doing, Becky. If he doesn't get some poison out of you, you'll die within hours," Trent said. He grabbed Becky's leg. "Go ahead. Do what you have to do, Pat."

Pat quickly cut an X across the snakebite. He bent down and pressed his mouth against the bleeding ankle and sucked. He spat a mouthful of blood onto the grass and then another.

Becky gritted her teeth and didn't cry out.

"That's the best I can do, Trent," Pat said when he finished. "She needs to see a doctor as soon as possible. They have snakebite remedy, ammonia."

"How do you know that?" Wes asked.

"I read too. Read it in a newspaper in Austin, Texas," Pat said.

"I'll saddle our horses," Trent said.

Bruce rushed up. "What happened?"

"Pa, a rattlesnake bit Becky on the ankle," Wes said.

"My Lordy me!" Bruce shouted. He grabbed Trent's shoulder. "What are we going to do?"

"I'm taking her to Council Grove. Pat sucked as much of the poison out as he could. But she needs to see a doctor. Pat said they could use ammonia on the snakebite."

"But she can't ride. She might lose consciousness and fall off her horse," Bruce protested.

"I'll tie her in the saddle. One horse can't carry the both of us all the way to Council Grove, at least not fast enough," Trent said.

"I'm going too," Wes said as he hurried after Trent.

"Okay," Trent said, not wanting to waste time arguing with the kid.

"You must save Becky," Bruce whispered.

"I will!" Trent said before he sprinted back to the wagons. He grabbed his saddle from under the wagon and ran out to where Tex grazed with the other hobbled horses. Within a few minutes Trent had Tex saddled. He hurried to saddle Becky's Morgan mare. On his way back, Wes joined him with Major.

"Help her up into the saddle," Trent called out from astride Tex as he led Becky's mare up to the group surrounding Becky.

"Please save her," Lois said as she wiped her cheeks.

"I'll get her to the doctor in Council Grove as fast as possible, Miss Lois. Hopefully, the doctor can help," Trent said. "Pat, help her into the saddle and then tie her feet in the stirrups."

"How do you feel," Lois asked her daughter as Becky mounted the mare.

"Lightheaded, Mama. And my ankle hurts something awful."

"It's going to be all right, sugar. Trent is gonna get you to the doctor as fast as he can," Lois added.

"Pat," Trent called out as he shifted his Sharps into the crook of his arm while his brother tied the girl's feet into the stirrups. "You look after the wagons. And I'll see you in Council Grove in two days."

"Good luck, Trent. She's got a lot of poison still in her," Pat said softly. "You got to get her to the doctor fast."

"Yup, I will," Trent added as Pat handed him the reins to Becky's horse. He turned in the saddle. "Wes watch your sister. If she slumps over the side of her horse, she might hurt herself."

"Sure thing, Trent.

"Let's ride!" Trent called out as he urged Tex into a gallop.

Chapter Sixteen
Council Grove

"Wes, take the horses to the livery stable we passed on the way into town," Trent said as he untied Becky's feet and lifted the semi-conscious girl out of the saddle. He glanced down at Lobo. "You stay outside," he ordered. The big dog stopped on the porch and watched Trent carry Becky to the door of the doctor's office.

"Where are we?" Becky mumbled weakly as Trent opened a door that had "Doctor Graham" written in bold black letters across it.

He managed to hold the girl with one hand while he opened the door with the other. "In Council Grove," Trent said as he stepped inside.

"Yes?" a man with a gray beard said as he laid the newspaper on the top of his desk. "What do we have here?"

Trent glanced around for a place to put Becky. "Snakebite!"

The man pointed at the table across the room. "How long ago?"

"Daybreak."

"Rattlesnake?" the doctor asked.

"Yup. On her ankle. My brother cut the wound and sucked some poison out," Trent replied while he carried Becky over to the table. He laid her down as gently as he could manage.

"If your brother hadn't worked on the snakebite, she'd be dead by now," the doctor said as he proceeded to a washbasin. "I've got a new remedy, but it could kill her instead of saving her," the doctor said while he dried his hands.

"Ammonia?"

The man stared over the wire rim of his spectacles.

"My brother read about it in a newspaper," Trent explained.

"Did he now?" the doctor said as he brought over a black bag and set it on the table beside Becky's head. "It's dangerous. I must open a vein in her arm and inject some ammonia into her. If I give her too much, it'll kill her. Too little and the venom will kill her."

"Doc, you best make sure you inject just the right amount." Trent snapped.

"So she means a lot to you? Are you two engaged to be married? I don't see a wedding ring."

"Nope. She... she's just a friend."

"What's that?" Trent asked when the doc pulled a metal cylinder with a pointed end from his black bag.

"A syringe. It was invented recently by an Irish doctor named Francis Rynd." He walked over to a shelf and opened a bottle. He stuck the pointed end of the cylinder into the bottle and pulled back on the plunger. "I just loaded it with ammonia. Now I've got to put some into her arm." He paused to look at Trent. "Hmm, I think, son, you want more than to just be her friend," the man said as he pulled a small all-metal knife out of his black bag. He grabbed Becky's right arm and reached down with the knife.

"Stop!" Trent yelled.

"Get that pistol out of my face!" the doctor yelled. "Do you want me to give her the ammonia remedy or not?" He took a deep breath. "I have to cut her vein open to inject the ammonia. It will bleed like the dickens, but it won't hurt her. I'll bandage her arm to stop the bleeding. I'm only going to make a small cut," he explained. "Now, put your gun away."

Reluctantly, Trent holstered his Colt. "I don't like you cutting her."

"I don't give a spit in the wind what you like or don't. Grab her arm and hold it still.

Becky moaned when Doctor Graham made the small incision in her arm. Trent flinched when blood squirted out from the cut. He watched as the doc placed the small end of the syringe into the cut and pushed down the plunger.

"That's it!" the doctor said as he grabbed a cloth bandage from his bag and started wrapping it around Becky's arm.

"Will it work?" Trent asked.

"We'll soon see!"

Becky suddenly kicked out with her injured leg. Then she sat up on the table and glanced around. "Where am I?"

"Lie back, child. You're in my office in Council Grove. I'm Doctor Graham. I just treated your snakebite with some ammonia. How do you feel?"

"A little dizzy and sleepy," Becky said as she laid back down on the table.

Doctor Graham placed a pillow under Becky's head. "Just lie there and rest, child." He motioned Trent over to his desk.

"She needs some bed rest. I am going to give her something to make her sleep."

"Is there a hotel nearby?" Trent asked.

"Yeah, about four blocks up the street. The Plainsman."

Trent turned toward the door. "I'll go and get a room. Take good care of her until I get back, Doc."

"Whoa there, sonny," a big burly man wearing a bowler hat said as Trent rushed out the door and collided with him.

"Sorry," Trent said quickly. "I didn't see you." Trent stepped aside. Lobo walked over, looked up at the man, and growled. Trent glanced down at Lobo. "He doesn't like strangers," he added and took a step toward the street.

"Hold up, sonny. Maybe you can save me from disturbing the good doctor," the man with acne scars said. He frowned at Lobo. "Just hold your dog off me for a moment."

"I'm in a hurry, sir," Trent replied.

"I saw you carry a blond-haired girl into the doctor's office. She resembled my cousin Gail Reddy. I hope nothing bad happened to my cousin. We just arrived from the east."

"No, the girl's name is Becky Cowan. We're on a wagon train. She got bit by a snake. I rode ahead to take her to the doctor. Now, if you will, sir, I need to finish my errand."

The man nodded. "Of course. And thank you for relieving my mind. I was worried sick when I saw you run into the doctor's office. I surely thought it was my cousin you carried in your arms," the man said and tipped his hat.

Trent had gone only a block when Wes caught up with him, winded from running. "I spotted you coming out of the doctor's office. How is Becky?" he added as he handed Trent his Sharps.

"I think she's going to be fine. I'm going to get a hotel room. The doc said she needs bedrest," Trent said.

"Should I go and sit with her until you get back?" Wes asked.

Trent shook her head. "No, she's asleep. No need to bother her. Come on with me."

"I saw you talking to someone in front of the doctor's office. What was that about?" Wes said as they continued toward the hotel.

"Some tenderfoot from back east thought Becky was his cousin," Trent said. "Dang it. I wish it had been the dandy's cousin and not Becky. I couldn't bear it if something happened to your sister," Trent said.

"Yup, I've seen how you look at Becky."

Trent shook his head. "Ah, don't tell your pa what I just said."

"He's got eyes too," Wes said as they climbed the steps to the Plainsman Hotel.

"I guess I'll get two rooms—one for Becky and one for you. I'll sleep in front of Becky's door," Trent said when they walked into a lobby filled with a red velvet sofa and overstuffed chairs. "Hmm, kind of fancy."

"Just get one room. We can sleep on the floor in Becky's room," Wes said as they approached the counter.

The man dressed in a black suit looked at Trent and Wes as though they were poor relatives begging for kitchen handouts.

"We need a room, sir," Trent said.

"There's a boarding house down the street that might suit your needs better, sir," the clerk said with a sneer.

"No, your establishment will do just fine," Trent said as he shifted his buffalo rifle in the crook of his arm.

"We don't take dogs!"

"You do now!" Trent said. "Now, why don't you fetch us a key to one of your rooms before my dog takes a pee on your leg or worse."

"Hmm," the desk clerk said as he turned around and grabbed a key off the peg. "That will be two dollars," he said, holding the key in his hand.

Trent reached into his dungarees and pulled out a gold piece. He flipped it onto the counter. "Three nights."

The clerk lifted the coin and bit into it to make sure it was real. "Here," he said and pushed the key across the counter. "And you'll have to put your X in the registration book," he added and pointed to an open ledger on the desk and a fountain pen. "Be careful with the pen. Press lightly, or it will make a blotch."

Trent lifted the pen and wrote his name smoothly. "I've used one before," he said and winked at the clerk. "Now, the key."

"It's room two hundred four. It's to the right, at the head of the stairs."

"Should we go to the room first?" Wes asked.

"No, let get back to the doctor's office. Becky might be awake and confused." Trent noticed the dirty look the desk clerk gave Lobo as they turned to leave.

"I think he likes Lobo more than you, Trent," Wes said and chuckled.

"Then he's smarter than I give him credit for," Trent replied.

"When will Pa and the wagons arrive?" Wes asked as they approached the doctor's office.

"Maybe tomorrow night," Trent said as they climbed the steps to the office. He opened the door and stopped in his tracks. The table was empty. He glanced over at the doctor, who again was busy reading his newspaper. "Where's Becky?"

"Her cousin fetched her," Doctor Graham said. "And he paid her bill."

"Cousin? She ain't got no cousin in Council Grove!" Trent shouted. "Wait a moment. Did the man who fetched her have a pitted face?"

"Yeah, must have had a bad case of acne when he was a youngster," the doc said as he pulled on his beard.

"Did he give his name?" Wes asked in a sudden shrill tone.

"Yeah, Mathias Coruthers," the doctor said.

"Dang it!" Wes swore. "That's the thug we left Boston to get away from. He wanted to marry Becky! He's the leader of the Boston shipyard gang."

Trent slapped his hat against his dungarees. "Goldarn it! Bruce warned me about him. He said he thought he had spotted him in Independence before the wagon train left. I should have recognized the man. He had a Boston accent and, for heaven's sake, an ugly face!"

Wes shook his head. "Don't beat yourself up, Trent. You had other things on your mind."

"Where did he take her?" Trent demanded as he took a step toward the doctor.

Doctor Graham shuddered when he saw the look on Trent's face. "He didn't say. Maybe the hotel?"

"No! We just came from the hotel!" Trent growled.

"There are some boarding houses. Maybe one of them?"

Trent started hard at the doctor. "Did you see his horse?"

"I glanced out the window. A bunch of men were waiting for him. Mister Coruthers had two of the men help the girl up into the saddle with him. He rode a gray gelding."

"Okay, that's something to go on," Trent said. "Come on, Wes, let's see if you can spot the gelding."

Lobo met them at the door. Trent patted him on the head.

"I wish your dog could track Becky," Wes said.

"He could if he knew that's what we wanted," Trent said. "You take one side of the street, and I'll take the other. Call me if you spot the gray gelding. Don't charge ahead on your own."

Wes didn't respond as he turned and walked across the street.

Trent shook his head. "He's as hard-headed as a stump."

Men in buckskin and beaver hats passed Trent. However, he also encountered settlers in dungarees with women wearing bonnets and calico dresses, driving ox-drawn covered wagons heading to the west end of town where the wagon trains assembled. That's where he would meet up with Bruce and the others.

As Trent searched the hitching post for the gelding, he kept an eye across the street on Wes. He feared if the kid spotted the gelding, he would try to take on the Boston thug and his gang members alone. And Trent dang sure didn't want to be responsible for getting Wes shot.

By the time he reached the wagon yard, Trent had wished he had fetched Tex instead of walking. Wes also seemed to be walking gingerly when they met.

Trent shook his head. "Nothing."

"I didn't see anything either," Wes said. "What do we do now?"

"I passed the sheriff's office. I guess we'll have to jaw with him a bit. Maybe he can help. Anyway, we have to tell him about Curt Cutler's gang in the dry wash east of here."

Wes nodded. "Yeah, I reckon we do. But I still don't cotton to the sheriff and his deputies claiming the reward money on those polecats when you and Pat did all the dirty work."

"It's blood money, Wes. Neither Pat nor I want it."

"It would go a long way toward Pa's dream of a homestead."

"Your father wouldn't accept bounty money, and you know it."

"Yeah, I guess you're right."

"There's the sheriff's office. Let's go and see if he can help locate Becky," Trent said. As they climbed onto the porch, Trent pointed to the floor. "Lobo, stay."

"He minds well," Wes said.

"Yeah, well, someone else trained him. I sure would like to know what happened to the fellow who owned him."

Chapter Seventeen
Mathias Coruthers

The slim man sitting behind the desk glanced between his boots at Trent and Wes when they walked through the door. He gave no greeting nor did he take his feet off the desk. He just stared at them as he puffed on his cigarillo.

"Are you the sheriff or deputy?" Trent asked as he approached the desk.

The man in the tan shirt tapped his finger on his badge. "Read it, if you can."

"Sheriff," Wes said with a sneer. "Maybe it should say deputy," he added.

"Maybe you should turn around and leave my office," the sheriff said as he tipped his hat back a little. "I'm not a member of the chamber of commerce."

Trent stepped in front of Wes. "Sheriff, we have a problem that you might be able to help us with."

The sheriff shook his head. "Yeah, well, I'm not inclined to help you. Tell me something that'll change my attitude."

"I brought in Wes's sister. She got bitten by a snake. Doc Graham patched her up, and I went to get a hotel room so she could rest. When I returned to the doctor's office, a man claiming to be her cousin had taken her while I was away."

Wes shook his head. "It wasn't my sister's cousin. It was a lowdown thug named Mathias Coruthers, who pursued my sister from Boston to force her to marry him!"

The sheriff smiled. "And I guess the blond here wants to marry her instead."

Trent stiffened.

"No, he and his brother are escorting our wagon train to California," Wes said.

"Yeah, sure he is, and he doesn't have an eye for your sister," the sheriff said and chuckled.

"Sheriff, watch what comes out of your mouth next," Trent said in a cold tone as he shifted the Sharps in the crook of his arm.

"Are you threatening me, boy?"

"Yup."

The sheriff locked eyes with Trent.

"Sheriff, if you say something that disrespects my sister, I'll shoot you between the eyes," Wes said. When the sheriff broke eye contact to look at Wes, the kid snatched his pistol out of his holster, held it pointed at the sheriff for a split second, and then twirled it back into his holster. "You get my drift."

The man behind the desk removed his feet from his desk and sat up straight in his chair. "I could throw you in jail for what you just did, kid."

Wes smiled. "You could die too."

Trent cleared his throat. "I think we all got off on the wrong foot. We came here seeking help in finding a girl kidnapped from Doc Graham's office. Now, maybe you're just in a bad mood, but you're the law here in Council Grove. We're asking for your help to find Becky."

The sheriff looked over at Wes. "Kid, if you weren't so darn fast on the draw, I would pull down your britches and give you a whipping."

"But you never have seen someone draw a pistol as fast as me," Wes said with a smile.

"God's truth, son," the sheriff said. He turned his gaze to Trent. "Describe this, Mathias Coruthers.

"Big guy with acne scars. He wears a bowler hat and has a Boston accent like the kid here."

"I've seen him in the Stampede Saloon. He had several dandies with him, each wearing shoulder holsters. I took them for Pinkerton men. But I guess they could be part of his Boston gang if what you're saying is true."

"Do you know where he's hanging his hat?" Trent asked.

"Nope, I didn't feel the need to jaw with him. I figured it might not be healthy for one of us. But if you mosey over to the saloon, I'm sure Polly might have the information you're looking for. He was hot to trot for her girls. Took a couple with him when he left the saloon."

Trent tipped his hat. "Thanks for the information. Ah, by the way, have you heard of a Texan outlaw named Curt Cutler?"

"Yes, I have. There are wanted posters on him and his men. Course, I value my life too much to go chasing after him. He's a mighty curly wolf. Why have you tangled with him and his gang?"

Wes spoke up before Trent could answer the question. "He sure has. He and his brother Pat killed half the gang. The other half is unarmed and afoot in a dry wash less than a day's ride east on the Santa Fe Trail."

The sheriff glanced at Trent. "Is that true?"

"Yup. They were going to attack our wagon train, so my brother and I stole their horses, and then when they tried to attack the wagons on foot, we picked them off with our rifles." Trent paused. "We hated to shoot them like buffalos, but they would have massacred the wagon train."

"From what I've heard of the gang, they surely would have killed every last one in the wagons," the sheriff agreed. "I guess y'all just made a handsome sum in bounty money."

Trent shook his head. "No, we don't want the bounty. You and your deputies can collect it." He nodded to Wes. "Let's mosey over to the saloon and jaw with Polly."

"Thanks for the tip about Curt Cutler and his gang," the sheriff called out as Trent walked through the door.

"He doesn't deserve the bounty money," Wes said as they walked onto the porch. "Unless they pay him in buffalo chips," he added with a chuckle.

"Curt Cutler is a curly wolf. I suspect he'll have a couple of surprises waiting for the good sheriff. He just might have to earn that bounty money," Trent said. "Do you remember which way to the saloon?"

Wes nodded. "It's down near the livery stable."

"Come on, Lobo," Trent called out as he headed down the street with determined strides. "You know, Wes, I'm going to send your Boston gangster to boot hill as surely as God made apples."

"Be careful. Mathias has killed a lot of men, according to Pa. He's quick drawing the .38 Colt from his shoulder holster," Wes said.

"Duly noted," Trent mumbled as they approached the saloon.

"From the horses at the hitching post, they have a crowd," Wes said.

Trent stopped and looked at Wes. "Dang it. I bet this is your first time in a saloon!"

"So what? I can't help that Pa wouldn't allow me in a bar in Boston. Boston seems years away!" Wes exclaimed. He glanced down at Lobo as they approached the butterfly doors. "Are you going to let Lobo enter?"

"Yup, he didn't like that Mathias guy when I ran into him on Doc Graham's porch. He might lead me to him if he gets his scent in the saloon."

The piano player didn't seem to be playing a song, just banging as hard as he could on the keyboard. However, that didn't keep prospectors and trappers from kicking up their heels with women in low-cut dresses or with each other. Except for a man in a gray suit sitting alone at the poker table, no one noticed their entrance.

"A game of poker?" the gambler asked as Trent approached.

"I don't play, but my dog does," Trent said. "And he's got plenty of fleas to put in the pot."

The man eyed Lobo and shook his head. Wes glanced at Trent with a puzzled look.

"I don't like gamblers," Trent said as he headed to a vacant space at the bar.

"There ain't no buffalos in here," said the bartender, a man with a face full of scars, as he nodded toward the Sharps.

"It's good for varmints too," Trent said as he lifted the rifle from the crook of his arm and leaned it against the bar. "I'm sure there's a lot of them here."

The bartender sighed and shook his head. "What do you and the boy want to drink?"

"Whiskey for me and sarsaparilla for the boy," Trent replied.

Wes shook his head. "No, whiskey for me too."

The bartender raised his eyebrows.

Trent shrugged. "If that's what he wants."

"Just don't puke," the bartender said as he pulled a bottle of whiskey and two shot glasses from under the bar.

"Which one of these lovely ladies is Polly?" Trent asked while the bartender poured the whiskey.

The bartender nodded toward a table near the bar. "She's the redhead sitting with those two Eastern tenderfoots."

"Are they from Boston?" Trent asked.

"Do I look like a booking agent?" the bartender said as he scooped up the coins Trent put on the bar.

"Not unless you're booking trips to hell," Trent said.

The bartender chuckled. "I like a man with a sense of humor. But they're rather short-lived."

Trent nodded. "Yeah, it does have its drawbacks," he said as he lifted his whiskey. He turned to face Wes. "Remember what the bartender said, don't puke." He touched his glass to Wes's and then threw the whiskey into the back of his mouth.

Wes did the same and instantly spit a mouthful of whiskey in the direction of the bartender. He wiped his mouth with the back of his sleeve. "Well, I didn't puke."

Trent tossed some money on the bar. "Try again, kid, while I walk over and have a few words with Miss Polly." Trent didn't wait to see if Wes agreed. He turned and walked determinedly over to the table the bartender had pointed out to him.

The redhead glanced up with a smile when Trent approached the table.

One of the men at the table, a younger and more handsome version of Mathias Coruthers, looked annoyed. "Move along, boy. The lady is busy."

"You sound like you're from Boston, pardner," Trent said.

"It ain't none of your business where I hail from. Now head for the hills, as they say, hereabouts."

"I have an acquaintance in Boston. Maybe you've heard his name. Mathias Coruthers. He sort of works at the Boston shipyards, if you get my drift," Trent said.

Lobo, who followed Trent over to the table, growled.

"You best get that mongrel out of my face before I put a bullet in him," the man said.

"Why are you looking for Mathias?" the redhead asked.

"I saw him earlier. He said he was looking for a scout to locate some friends of his from Boston. Told me to stop by and jaw with him about a job."

The man who resembled Mathias shook his head. "Uncle Mathias didn't tell me anything about no scout."

"Hmm, I guess your uncle doesn't tell you everything," Trent said.

The man started to rise from his chair.

"Travis," one of the other men called out. "You know Mathias is looking for the family too. The kid is probably telling the truth about him offering a scouting job."

"Keep your pie hole shut, Terry."

Terry nodded.

"Are you going to take me to your uncle or not?" Trent said. "If not, then I'll get back to the bar with my brother."

Travis glanced at the bar. "He don't look like you."

Trent nodded. "Lucky for him, he takes after our ma."

Travis took a deep breath. "Okay, come on, boys, let's take him and his brother to see Uncle Mathias.

Polly pointed her finger at Travis. "Tell Mathias he better not make a mess of the house. The girls' customers like it neat."

Travis stood and stared down at the redhead. "It's a cathouse. It's a mess already."

"Just mind what I said, or you'll be out of the cathouse tonight, big guy," Polly said in a softer tone.

Travis ignored Miss Polly. "Come on, let's go," he told Trent.

"What kind of cats do they raise in this part of the country?" Wes whispered to Trent as they followed Travis and his two companions across the saloon.

"The kind that wears low-cut dresses," Trent replied.

"Oh!" Wes said.

"Leave the mongrel!" Travis said as they walked out onto the porch of the saloon.

"Nope, he's my tracker. He goes with me, or I don't go," Trent said.

"Okay, but if he craps on the porch, I'll shoot him," Travis said as he climbed down the steps.

"Do we need our horses?" Wes asked.

"Children should be seen and not heard," Travis said.

Trent noticed how Wes suddenly tensed up, so he placed his hand on Wes's shoulder.

"No, the house is only a block away," Travis said.

"What do you all do in Boston?" Trent asked.

"We mind our own business," Travis said. "And just so you know, my uncle likes questions even less than I do. You best keep your lips together unless he asks you a question."

"Thanks for the advice," Trent said in a lighthearted tone.

"You sound pleased to get a job," Terry, who walked beside Trent, said.

"Yeah, I don't like unfinished business," Trent said as they turned into the yard of an unpainted high-gabled, two-story house with a porch the length of the front of it.

"Terry, you and Buster keep the boy company on the porch while I take the scout in to see Uncle Mathias. The mongrel stays on the porch."

"No, your uncle likes Lobo. He'll want to see him again," Trent said.

"Well, for the dog's sake, I hope you're right, or else he'll shoot him," Travis said as he opened the door.

"No, he won't shoot Lobo," Trent said as he winked at Wes when he passed by.

"Uncle Mathias!" Travis called out. "I brought the scout you wanted to talk to."

"Scout? What in blazes are you talking about?" a deep gruff voice replied from upstairs, followed by heavy footsteps.

Travis turned to glance at Trent and found a buffalo rifle pointed at him. Trent kept the rifle aimed at Travis as he backed out of view of the stairs. "If he asks you, tell him I'm waiting on the porch, if you want to live."

Travis swallowed.

"You know better than to bring a stranger to me, Travis," Mathias shouted as he walked down the stairs.

"I... I made him stay on the porch, Uncle."

"What in tarnation caused you to bring him here in the first place?" Mathias said as he walked into the room. "And why are you standing there like you have a corncob shoved up your rear?"

"Howdy again," Trent said as he swung his rifle to cover Mathias. Lobo growled.

"I see you brought your mangy flea hotel with you," Mathias said.

"Where's Becky?" Trent demanded.

"My God, Uncle Mathias, I didn't realize he's with her," Travis said and turned pale.

"I've got seven armed men upstairs. One word from me and they'll come running down the stairs," Mathias said.

"I'll kill them all," Trent said in a calm voice. "And you first."

"You got salt, boy, to confront me," Mathias joked. "I'm going to take my time with you. I ain't gonna let you die too quick."

Trent switched his Sharps to cover Travis. "The next words out of your mouth better be for your men to bring Becky downstairs, or I'm going to put a big hole in your nephew's belly, and then I'm going to draw my Colt and shoot you between the eyes."

"Now, boy, I don't doubt you can shoot Travis, but I seriously doubt you're fast enough to drop that rifle and beat me to the draw," Mathias said.

"Lobo!" Trent called the wolf-dog's name.

The beast lowered itself until its belly almost touched the floor as he stalked across the room toward Mathias.

"You were saying?" Trent said as Lobo inched forward. "Which one of us are you going to try to shoot after I kill Travis? You just might get one of us, but not both. Either I shoot you or Lobo rips your throat out. You'll have to choose which way you die. Now, that's in case I'm too slow on the draw. Otherwise, I shoot you in the belly, and Lobo rips your throat out."

Mathias shook his head. "Son, you do like to hear yourself talk."

"Yeah, I inherited it from my father. He could talk the hide off a cow," Trent said as he watched Mathias's eyes. He must have seen something because he swung his rifle around and shot the big, ugly man in the belly as Lobo leaped into the air. Still holding his rifle in his left hand, Trent drew his Colt. He beat Travis to the draw and shot him between the eyes.

Shouting erupted from upstairs, and two shots rang out from the porch. As men rushed downstairs, Wes stepped inside the house with his pistol smoking. He nodded at Trent before glancing up as the first man appeared on the stairs. The boy shot him and the next three men. Out of ammo, he nodded at Trent, who took his place and put a bullet in the fifth man and sixth man. The last man dropped his pistol and raised his hands.

"Don't shoot?" he yelled.

"Where's the girl?"

"She's upstairs locked in her room," the man said nervously.

"If she's been harmed in any way, you're a dead man," Trent said as he headed up the stairs. "Show me where she is."

"She's fine. No one has touched her, not even Mister Coruthers. The doc gave her something to make her sleep. She's still asleep," the man said.

"You darn sure better be telling me the truth, pilgrim, or else I'll shoot you in the gut and leave you for my dog to finish.

The man glanced down at Lobo, still worrying Mathias's body, and cringed. "I ain't lying. Sure as God is my witness."

As they reached the top of the stairs, the man took a key out of his pocket and walked over to the third room. He unlocked the door and stepped back. Trent opened the door and peeked inside. Becky lay in a four-poster bed on a feather mattress with a blissful look on her face.

"Head for the hills before I shoot you," Trent turned and said. "Wes let this polecat go. When he gets back to Boston, he'll have a good story to tell."

"Are you sure, Trent?"

"Yup, I am," Trent said as he walked into the room. He paused before advancing to the side of the bed. "Becky!" The girl's facial expression didn't change. "Becky, wake up!" Trent added as he grabbed her arm and shook her.

"What!" Becky's eyes snapped open. She sat up. "What's going on? Where am I, and why am I in this bed?"

"You got bit by a rattlesnake. Do you remember that?" Trent asked.

"Yeah, and... and you took me to Council Grove. I vaguely remember an old man with a beard hovering over me. That's all I remember." She glanced at her arm. "Why is my arm bandaged?"

"Come on. We have to go. I'll explain everything once we get to the hotel. I'm pretty sure it might not be safe to linger here. You were kidnapped by a man named Mathias Coruthers. He might have other men we don't know about in town."

"Oh my. He followed us all this way?"

"Yeah, well, he won't follow you any farther. He's dead, and so are all of his men, except for the one I let go," Trent said as he helped Becky out of bed. "Can you walk on your bad leg?"

Becky glanced down. "Look, the swelling is gone. It hurts some, but I can manage. Is the hotel far?"

"About four blocks," Trent said as Becky leaned against him while she walked to the door. "Oh, there are several dead men on the stairs and down on the floor."

"Hi, sis!" Wes called out as he waved.

"Becky, I'm sorry you have to see this," Trent said as they walked by Mathias's dead men. "Wes and I had to kill them. There was no way around it."

Becky put her hand over her mouth. "Is that Mathias Coruthers over there?"

"Lobo, that's enough!" Trent said.

The big wolf-dog stopped growling, looked up, and wagged his tail.

"He's happy to see you, Becky," Trent said as Becky walked gingerly to the door.

"Yeah, I think I want to keep on his happy side."

Epilogue

"Pa, I can't believe they voted you the wagon train master," Wes said as he helped his father hitch up the oxen to the wagon. All around them, men and women were getting ready for the trail. Wes counted fifty wagons assembled in the wagon yard of Council Grove. Most were drawn by oxen, but several had teams of mules. Marty and Grace worked, getting Bruce's second wagon hooked up to the team of oxen. Bruce had given them half the space in the wagon to store their belongings.

"I wouldn't have been chosen if Trent hadn't turned down the job and asked that they vote for me. He promised to be my lieutenant. That's what sealed the election for me. And to be honest, Wes, I wouldn't have taken the job if Trent hadn't promised to be the second in command. I'm still too green to command a big wagon train across the dangerous ground we still have to cover."

"Pa," Becky called out as she climbed off the seat of the wagon. "Where's Trent?"

Bruce smiled at his daughter. He had come close to losing her. Bruce didn't like killing, but he was glad Trent and Lobo had put Coruthers in the dirt. "He and Pat are going around the yard, seeing if anyone needs help to hitch their teams.

He should be back soon." Even as Bruce spoke, he heard a galloping horse. He turned around. "Here he comes now."

Becky smiled as she watched Trent rein Tex to a stop a few feet away.

"Morning, Miss Becky. How are you feeling this morning?" Trent said as he dismounted.

"My arm is still sore where that old coot of a doctor cut me."

"He saved your life, I reckon," Trent said and smiled.

"Wes finally told me what went down at the house when you rescued me," Becky said.

Trent lowered his head to stare at the ground. "Shucks, it was nothing. I sent some men to boot hill who needed to make the trip. You know gunplay comes naturally to Pat and me."

"Yeah, I can't seem to turn the corner on that fact," Becky said as she frowned momentarily. "However, you're the reason I'm still alive."

Lobo walked up and sniffed Becky's ankle.

"I must admit, seeing your dog shaking Coruthers scared the bejeebers out of me at the time," Becky said before reaching down and patting Lobo on the head. "However, like some people, animals are vicious only when they need to be."

"Hey," Wes shouted from the far side of the team of oxen. "I helped save you from Coruthers too, sis."

"Yes, yes, and you keep reminding me," Becky replied.

"Well, I better get back to checking the wagons. I just spotted you coming out and thought I would ride over and say hi," Trent said as he turned to mount Tex.

"Wait," Becky said.

Trent turned back around. "What?"

"This," Becky said as she stepped forward and planted a quick kiss on Trent's cheek. Before Trent could react, Becky turned and walked back to the wagon.

Trent glanced at Bruce, who was staring at him from in front of the team of oxen. He turned red. "Bruce, I didn't. I don't know why..."

"It's fine with me, Trent. Now get back to checking the wagons," Bruce said and smiled.

"Yes, sir. Right away," Trent called out happily as he vaulted onto the back of Tex.

The End

Thanks for taking the time to read this story. A positive review on Amazon would be appreciated.

Made in the USA
Monee, IL
28 January 2021

58925144R00100